Jon grew up in South Kent on a steady diet of hammer horror, punk rock and Ready Brek. He found success with his band, The Filth FC, and later went on to join street punk legends, The Business, playing major venues all over the world.

He then worked for record labels and dabbled in music journalism. However, he found his calling when he quit everything to care for his disabled daughter, Izzy. They moved to the USA until Izzy's passing at the age of eighteen.

Now, he lives in the middle of nowhere in Kent with his loud son, Henry, and his wife and best friend, CJ.

You can occasionally find him being rude to the regulars in a gorgeous country pub where he works and gets all his weirdest ideas from.

Seriously, the locals are weird.

For Izzy, for everything.

For Henry. I hope this makes you as proud of me as I am of you every day.

For CJ, for the love, patience and Toblerone.

Jon C. Trickey

GREATEST HITS VOLUME 1

AUSTIN MACAULEY PUBLISHERS™
LONDON • CAMBRIDGE • NEW YORK • SHARJAH

Copyright © Jon C. Trickey 2024

The right of Jon C. Trickey to be identified as author of this work has been asserted by the author in accordance with sections 77 and 78 of the Copyright, Designs and Patents Act 1988.

All rights reserved. No part of this publication may be reproduced, stored in a retrieval system, or transmitted in any form or by any means, electronic, mechanical, photocopying, recording, or otherwise, without the prior permission of the publishers.

Any person who commits any unauthorised act in relation to this publication may be liable to criminal prosecution and civil claims for damages.

This is a work of fiction. Names, characters, businesses, places, events, locales, and incidents are either the products of the author's imagination or used in a fictitious manner. Any resemblance to actual persons, living or dead, or actual events is purely coincidental.

A CIP catalogue record for this title is available from the British Library.

ISBN 9781035824236 (Paperback)
ISBN 9781035824250 (ePub e-book)
ISBN 9781035824243 (Audiobook)

www.austinmacauley.com

First Published 2024
Austin Macauley Publishers Ltd®
1 Canada Square
Canary Wharf
London
E14 5AA

None of this would have been possible without the continuing support and love from my family.

Thanks to Ella and the AM folk for getting me here.

To my friends who read and critiqued this old nonsense, I owe you a pint.

Table of Contents

Family Business	11
Dave the Grumpy Narwhal	31
Dave the Narwhal in the Hamster Club	38
Pramface	50
Nuts	70
Mr Greendale's Oak Tree	85
Invasive Species	101
A Stupid Old Tradition	127
A Guest for Dinner	139
Richard Jones	147

Family Business

The ornamental bell over the pub door jangled merrily as the door opened inwards. Keith the landlord looked up from his crossword, perched as he was on his throne, a requisitioned kitchen stool located behind the bar. He instantly recognised the honest faces and cheery grins of Ted and Stewart, his most irregular of regulars, as they stepped inside, shivering and shuddering and scampering to be out of the drizzle on a cold November night. Keith smiled instantly, genuinely pleased to see them, and commenced the pouring of two perfect pints of spitfire. Ted, the taller of the two, led the way to the bar and struggled out of his jacket before settling on a bar stool. Stewart was not far behind, and it was he that Keith addressed first.

"Stewart! Long time no see! Back from the wilds of the Highlands already?"

"Just got back now. Ted met me at the train station and we walked straight here, after dropping my case back home." Stewart smiled as his pint was placed reverently before him. "And might I say I'm bloody glad to be back. A week is way too long to be without a decent beer, for one thing, and furthermore, there was a great deal of unpleasantness." With that, he lifted his glass to his lips and swiftly drained a third of the liquid. "Ah, that's the stuff!" he exclaimed with a happy sigh.

"A week is equally too long to be away from your conversation, sir," Ted added as he fished a fiver from his front pocket and offered it to Keith before taking sup himself.

"So, did I miss anything exciting in my absence?" queried Stew, glancing around the familiar interior. It was as it always was, and always will be. The logs burnt welcomingly in the fireplace, above which the pub clock sliced time with an audible tick, judge, jury and executioner on the hotly debated matter of last orders. The walls were a deep red, and sported many a humorous print and horse brass. A bookshelf hung by the lavvy door, cluttered with well-thumbed paperbacks and the occasional board game. The carpet was dark, darker than it was when installed countless decades ago, the ghosts of a thousand spilt pints obscuring the original pattern, but hints of its former glory were still visible underneath the tables.

The tables themselves were an eclectic bunch, like their brethren, the chairs, mismatched, battle-scarred but comfortable. The bar itself was a great mahogany monstrosity, with glasses hanging from the top and stools crowding its bottom, so to speak. The single window was directly next to the door, latticed and swathed in thick velvety curtains, the co-conspirators in Keith's less than legal lock-in larks. All as it should be, and all as it would ever be.

"Nothing to report. Been a quiet week really. Quiet night too," Keith said as he returned to his stool. "Your two faces are the only ones I've seen all night." Ted and Stewart nodded in an unsurprised manner at this. Most nights they were the only clientele. "So, there's my update, you must tell us all about your Scottish adventure."

"Yes, this unpleasantness of which you speak sounds most intriguing. You've been suspiciously tight-lipped since I picked you up at the station. Visiting an uncle, wasn't it?" Ted added.

Stewart smiled the smile of the centre of attention and reached for his glass.

"Close. Visiting the estate of an uncle. Uncle Hamish, he died last month after a short illness. I, as the last remaining relative, was summoned to attend to various details following his death. And bloody weird it was too, I don't mind telling you."

"Weird, how so?" said Keith, his nose for drama quivering in anticipation. "Oh, and sorry for your loss, of course."

"No bother, Hamish and I weren't at all close. In fact, the first I heard he'd popped his clogs was when I got the message from his lawyer that I was needed up there last week. I would love to continue but sadly find my throat a little dry." Stewart waggled his empty glass in the direction of Keith.

"Yeah, and I would love to carry on listening but my ears are dry also," Ted added, his equally empty glass waggling in unison. Keith hopped off his perch and attended to the pints with his usual elan.

Drinks were replenished, payment given, change returned.

"Cor, that's the business," Stewart said on first swallow. "No spitfire up in the Highlands, you know."

"Barbaric," muttered Keith under his breath. "That's one of the many reasons I loathe travelling past Kent's boundaries."

"Anyway, so, I get the call late Thursday to leave immediately Friday morning for Goolie. Ticket all paid for, and everything," Stewart continued.

"Goolie?" Ted arched a brow.

"Yes, Goolie. A noble place of great antiquity, home to Uncle Hamish's country seat."

"Really? Sounds like the feed line for a very cheap joke to me."

"Well, it's not. May I continue?" Stewart inquired peevishly.

"Please do."

"Anyway, so, off I toddle to the train station with my suitcase Friday morning. Dull old ride up to the Highlands, but I had the foresight to pack a particularly gripping hardback and a sixer of spitfire from the supermarket, so it was a pleasant enough journey. I had to change at Ashford, though, of course."

"Of course," chorused Ted and Keith.

"Eventually, I get to Goolie Grove train station, where I was met by a driver hired by my uncle's lawyers to get me up to the big house. Seems as remote as Goolie is, Great Goolie Hall is even more so."

"Hold on, hold on, Great Goolie Hall? Are you sure this isn't a wind-up?" questioned Ted incredulously.

"Absolutely! If you are done insulting the moniker of my family's country estate, may I...?"

"Yes, of course, sorry."

They were interrupted by the jaunty jangle of the bell above the door, announcing the arrival of another customer. All three pairs of eyes surveyed the newcomer, a large bulky man, dressed for the drizzle in a dense dark duster. His heavy brows and bushy beard melded almost perfectly with the furry Russian hat that he had wedged on his oversized head. Ted and Stewart greeted him in the traditional English pub manner, by scrutinising him silently. Keith, the consummate professional, leapt into action and greeted the stranger from behind the bar.

"Beer," the stranger muttered tersely over his shoulder as he ignored the cheery greeting and headed straight to the table closest to the fire.

"Right you are, sir," Keith said to the man's back as he started pouring a pint of fizzy lager that had been out of date for years, solely reserved for customers who were rude and/or showed no preference in what beer they ordered.

Ted and Keith watched in silence as Keith delivered the pint of horrible lager to the table, received a crisp five-pound note, short-changed the stranger and returned to his stool.

"You know, Keith, if you didn't continually rip off prospective new customers and give them that crappy beer, you may get a few more regulars," observed Ted, sotto voce.

"And where would you be then, eh? No room at the bar, requests for a telly, ladies night promotions, all inexorably leading to the inevitable—karaoke nights. No thank you, I am happy with my system, and I suspect you are too," said Keith with a shudder.

"You have a point there," conceded Ted. "Perhaps having a few more people in here would not necessarily be a good thing."

"Anyway, where was I? Oh yeah. Great Goolie Hall," Stewart said, hastily drawing the attention back to his tale and himself. "So, I get to the house, late Friday night. Last time I was there I was just a sprog, I'd totally forgotten how massive it is. Huge, rambling country house, like you'd see on a BBC drama Sunday evening. There, waiting for me, was Morag, my uncle's housekeeper. She had been employed by him for about the last twenty years or so, and she looked like a prune in a mob cap, I don't mind telling you. The housekeeper I remembered from my youthful visit had been a saucy French piece, Mme Bonfils. She made quite the impact on my early pubescence, if you know what I mean." Ted and Keith both nodded sagely as Stewart continued, "Anyway, Morag had prepared a room and some dinner and let me know my uncle's lawyer would be there in the morning and left me to my own devices."

"Next day, after a slap-up breakfast, the lawyer, Mr Arberghast, showed up. Odd fellow, he looked like someone had contrived to animate dust and put it in a pinstripe suit. Anyway, long story short, as poor old Hamish's last living relative, I got everything." Stewart revelled in the identical looks of shock on Ted and Keith's faces.

"Wait, what?" sputtered Ted. "All to you? All of it?"

"Yup. Lock, stock and barrel."

"Holy crap."

"Indeed. More beer is called for, I think, don't you, Keith?" Beamed Stewart.

Keith stared at Stewart for a few moments, his mouth opening and closing in fair facsimile of a flounder. Fortunately his professionalism took over and he drew two pints from the pump in such a way that would make angels weep. Payment made, change received.

"Anyway, so, I was in quite a bit of a tizzy with the news, so old Arberghast said he'd give me time to process it all, look over the house and contents and whatnot, and he'd come back after the weekend with all the paperwork, and to talk over some complications."

"Complications?" Ted raised a quizzical brow.

"More on those later," Stewart said, glass en route to lips. "Anyway, so, I spent a happy Saturday exploring the place, having a poke in all the cupboards, you know. Some pretty fancy stuff, I can tell you. Armoires, credenzas, tuffets, fauteuils and even the odd klinai or two. Ornaments and antiques a go-go. I stopped for lunch on the veranda, then dinner in the great room.

"Morag isn't one for chitchat so I was left pretty much to my own devices. After dinner, I found the library and a drinks cabinet filled with my uncle's favourite tipple, gin. Well, the library has a fireplace, and before you know it, I was firmly ensconced in a chair, gin in hand, book open."

"Is it a drink cabinet that is disguised as a globe?" said Keith breathlessly.

"It is indeed."

"Ah, the very acme of style," Keith sighed happily.

"Quite so. So, I woke up Sunday morning in the armchair, somewhat calmer and more at ease with my sudden change in fortunes, but with a mildly muddy head from the gin. Morag came in and told me that I would have a guest for dinner that evening, my uncle's best friend, Binky," Stew continued.

"Binky?" Said Ted.

"Binky. Well, he's really Alasdair, ninth Earl of somewhere or other, but he goes by Binky. Toffs, you know how they are." All nodded in agreement. "So, I busy myself by walking the grounds, you know, that kind of thing. Anyway, Binky shows up, and he's a top bloke, about seventy I guess, green tweed suit, shock of thick white hair. Now all through dinner, he's very reserved, doesn't say much, but after we retire to the library and Morag finishes for the night, well, then his mouth starts to run away with him, and that's where the story gets interesting."

"As opposed to your everyday, run of the mill tale of a bloke down the pub who inherits a colossal country estate from an estranged uncle?" Keith interjected.

"Precisely," agreed Stewart. "Anyway, so we are in the library, fire burning away, gin in hand, when Binky tells me how long he knew Hamish for, how they were best friends, etcetera, etcetera. Establishing his credentials, I reckon. Anyway, first, he tells me that they were both a bit of a lad back in the day. You know, not only drinking and hell raising, but roistering AND doistering to boot."

Ted let out a whistle through his teeth. "Roistering AND doistering? Blimey."

"I know, right? Anyway, Binky tells me how in their younger days, back in their early twenties, neither of them could stand whisky, which was a bit of an anomaly for landed Scottish gents, but they both developed a love of gin, which is why, back then, they were known as," here Stewart paused for dramatic effect, "the gin gang of Goolie." Stewart looked at the other two expectantly. Ted looked at the floor, shaking his head. Keith winced in visible pain, rubbing the bridge of his nose between thumb and forefinger.

"No? Fine, suit yourselves," said grumpy Stewart in his best Frankie Howerd. "Anyway, terrible puns aside, Binky really started to open up to me. Turns out, as well as the usual drunken upper class stuff, you know, drunkenly riding a horse through a ballroom naked, firing cannonballs at the neighbours, that kind of standard stuff, old Hamish was a bit of a one for the ladies. What with his vast amount of money and his dashing good looks, he found that the ladies would, more often than not, reciprocate his attentions. Sadly, though, he was very much a love 'em and leave 'em type of chap, and hardly a Sunday morning would go by without some poor marchioness or minor royal being escorted from the estate in tears after Hamish was through with them."

"Well, word got around, and after a while the aristocratic ladies of the area got wise to him, and stopped trying to turn him into husband material. So, Hamish turned his attention to the ladies of the village, who soon cottoned on that hooking up with him was less of a chance to become a trophy wife and more of a chance to become a notch on the bedpost, so that source dried up too. Binky said Hamish was despondent and seriously started to think about settling down, you know, finding a suitable bride out of the rapidly diminishing pool of posh girls who had no idea of his free loving past. And then, fate intervened."

"Beer," said the man by the fire, without turning around. Keith shrugged in a 'what're you going to do' kind of way, and while he attended to the other customer, Ted and Stewart took the opportunity to visit the khazi. All tasks complete, the three reconvened at the bar.

"Anyway, where was I? Oh yeah, so, fate. What happened next, according to Binky, is my uncle met Lulu, or as I knew her as a child, Mme Bonfils." Stewart looked at the blank faces of the other two.

"Mme Bonfils? Hamish's original housekeeper?"

"Aah," exclaimed Ted and Keith in unison.

"Right? So, what had happened is, Hamish had met Lulu at some event or other and had fancied her straight off. Like I said, she was a stunner. Turns out, though, that she was more than a match for old unk, and after a few weeks, he found himself actually in love with her. Now, obviously a man of his standing could not get married to some commoner, a French one at that, so he installed her at Great Goolie Hall, where they lived as man and wife behind closed doors, but society saw them as toff and servant."

"A story as old as time," sighed Keith.

"Okay. So, by this time, it was pretty late Sunday night. Binky was pretty wasted on expensive booze, and I was feeling the effects. Apparently, he had a permanent room ready for him in the house should just such an occasion arise, and off he staggered, promising to finish the story the next day. So, next day arrives, Monday if you're keeping track. Binky rolls out of bed just before twelve, and after some food and a quick hair of the dog, we go for a stroll in the grounds, so Binky can finish off the story."

"He explained that all was copacetic with Uncle and Lulu for a good many years. The arrangement as they called it, was not ideal, but the best either could hope for, given the circumstances. Then, of course, things changed, as they are wont to do." Stewart looked longingly at his empty glass.

"Room for another there, you two?" Keith said, already halfway through pulling a fresh one.

"It's like watching Michelangelo paint a ceiling," said Ted, as he watched the master at work.

Swiftly, two perfectly poured pints were placed and paid for.

"So, what happened? What always happens." Stewart carried on after wiping beery foam from his top lip with his cuff. "Lulu got up the duff. Now, I only have Binky's account, and he was close with my uncle, so it may be biased but the way he told it was Hamish tried to do his best, given the situation. Obviously there was no way he could legitimise the child or the relationship, what with how things were back then, but he did offer to keep Lulu and the child in the house, in perpetuity, and while he couldn't acknowledge the child as his, he would make it the sole heir to the estate. This was not to Mme Bonfils' liking and she refused. She demanded that the child be brought up with all advantages and privilege due to it, and was disgusted that Hamish would even suggest that it remained, in her words a 'sale petit secret'—dirty little secret. Much furniture was thrown, many tears were shed, and, just a scant few weeks after she had discovered her condition, Lulu disappeared one night, never to return."

"Crikey," said Ted.

"It gets even weirder," Stew retorted. "So, as Binky is telling me this, we are walking back to the house across the back lawn. We see Morag walking quickly towards us. As soon as she sees us, she waves and tells me there's a phone call. While I take it, Binky excuses himself to partake of some gin in the library."

"Turns out, it's Mr Arberghast's office, wondering why he had not returned to the office yet, after our scheduled meeting that morning. Well, I had quite forgotten about that, what with the gin, and Binky, and the scandal and all, so I told them he had never arrived. They got quite worried about that, and because of Mr Arberghast's age and the windy roads leading up to the hall, they asked me if I could check that he had not had an accident or broken down. Well, I was pleased to help, and after informing Binky of the situation, he said he would love to help look for the old fellow with me."

"As it happens, it didn't take long at all. Found the car at the bottom of the drive, crashed into a tree. No sign of Arberghast, but the door had been ripped clean from its hinges. Well, old Binky goes deathly pale at this, and runs back to the house as fast as his elderly legs can take him, shouting that he was calling the police. I let him go and had a poke about in the undergrowth. A few seconds, and a partially flattened rhododendron later, I discover Arberghast."

"Dead?" said Ted.

"Dead, Ted," Stewart said.

"In a ghastly and eldritch manner?" squeaked Keith.

"You hit the nail on the head there, chief. Torn limb from limb. Great ghastly slashes, head torn off. Purpling innards pooling on the floor, the lot. Now, I'm not a medical man, but even I could see it was the work of some great beast, and when they arrived, the police confirmed it. First copper there, poor sod, chucked his guts up as soon as he saw it. So, the whole of the local constabulary turned up, both of them, and started beating the bushes, so to speak, trying to flush it out. Nothing. They took a statement from me, and a representative from Arberghast's firm arrived shortly afterwards."

"He confirmed the paperwork would need to be reprinted and resigned from his end, what with courts taking a fairly dim view of important papers covered in blood and innards and all that, and that would take a day or two. Under the circumstances, he wondered if I could come into town to sign and discuss further on Wednesday. Of course, I could oblige and arranged a time to be there. By now, it was late evening, and Morag had clocked off, leaving me dinner of liver and kidney, which I usually love, but found in quite bad taste, given the state of poor old Arberghast. No bother, I thought, and repaired to the library for a drink or two."

"There, propped up on my armchair, I found a note from Binky. I had quite forgotten about him in all the excitement and post homicide bureaucracy. Well, old Binky had been called back to his manor house on urgent business, but had news to impart. Could I meet him in a pub he knew, two towns over, Thursday evening? I admit I was curious and pencilled the time and place into my diary, before getting on with the real business of the evening, drinking Hamish's gin and enjoying the fire and books. I must have fallen asleep there again, because that's where I woke up the next morning."

"Bloody hell," gasped Keith. "This was Monday, as in four days ago?"

"Yup. So, I spend most of Tuesday morning wondering where the bloody hell my breakfast was. Morag didn't show up for work. I plodded down to the kitchen to fix myself a bacon sandwich and a cup of tea, and when I got there, guess what I found? Back door left wide open, by the looks of it all night. Well, I was bloody furious. Silly old mare left the back door unlocked after going home, with a vicious beast roaming the grounds? So I go to shut it, and that's where my day would've carried on as usual if I hadn't caught a glimpse of something in a tree out back. Off I traipse, across the damp grass in my socks, which, I think we can all agree, is the absolute worst." Ted and Keith murmured in agreement.

"And what do I see hanging in the tree? Morag's head. Well, not just her head, but a goodly bit of spine too. The rest of her was tossed into the bushes a few feet off. Looked like when your ice lolly falls off its stick, she did." Stewart took a swig of spitfire at this point. "So, back to the house, call the cozzers, out they come, questions, vomiting and more beating of the bush, you know the score by now. The officer in charge said they had very limited resources and were only just getting around to looking at old Arberghast, so it may be some time before they had any answers. I am not a medical man, he said, however it looked like a massive animal of some sort had de-nutted poor old Morag, leaving marks very similar to those on Arberghast."

"The likelihood of two vast predatory animals roaming around Goolie were slim, so they were working on the assumption it was the same creature. I expressed my windiness at the current situation and fears of a further attack, and the officer said they were diverting all the resources of the Goolie police to this, and both officers would be patrolling the woods sporadically. They were drafting officers from other areas to help, but they weren't available until after the weekend, apparently there was a wedding they'd both been invited to. Anyway, after all the fuss had finished, it was early evening, and frankly, seeing the filleted husk of Morag had put me off the idea of cooking for myself, I can tell you. So, I phoned for takeout."

"What sort of traditional Scottish fare did you dine on?" inquired Ted.

"Pad Thai, tom yam and a great green curry, from the takeout in the village, the Bangkok Kilt-on. Anyway, so after the delivery chap left, I locked up everything tight as a drum and availed myself of the spectacular gin in the library, as had become habit. Wednesday morning arrived, and as I waited for a taxi to come pick me up to take me into the village, I checked all the doors and windows. No sign of any scratches or marks."

"Well, I assumed the Goolie Ghoulie, as the villagers were calling the beast, had moved on to pastures new. I got into the village early, had a spot of lunch in the local pub, the Sassenach's Head, very nice, and went to my meeting at the lawyers. Well, the atmos there was pretty depressing, I can tell you. People blubbing and stuff, big picture of Arberghast in the lobby. I was there the whole afternoon, signing and dating, and by the end of it, I was the sole owner of Great Goolie Hall, its contents and lands, and a hefty bank balance to boot."

"The lawyer chap asked me my intentions, and I said I intended to keep the Hall in my possession. So, after all the paperwork was finished, I ambled back over the road to the Sassenach's Head and had a pint or two of the local brew to celebrate my newfound wealth. The locals were more curious than friendly, but they weren't hostile towards me, and by closing time, I was very happy with my lot. A quick cab ride later, I'm back in what's now my library, drinking my gin by my fire." Stewart finished up his pint, and Ted followed suit. The three agreed on a pee break, and presently they were reunited in front of a brace of crisp new pints.

"It's twenty minutes to last orders," observed Ted as they settled back into their stools, so to speak.

"I'm nearly done," said Stewart affably.

"Jolly good, because I'm sure I'm speaking for the pair of us when I say we have some bloody large questions about this whole affair," replied Ted, brow beetling, as Keith nodded in agreement. "Like for instance, bloody hell, what are you planning to do with a huge mansion? And are you rich now? Much less the plethora of doubts I have about all the plot holes."

"Never fear, all will be revealed. Thursday arrives, well, yesterday arrives, and I decided to travel to Binky's home town a trifle early, get a spot of lunch, check out their pubs, you know the score. So, off I pop in a cab, all the way to Little Balloch."

"I'm going to have to stop you there," groaned Ted. "These horribly forced puns are testing my patience."

"Quite so," Stew answered agreeably. "That's the last, I think. Anyway, I have a very enjoyable day, pottering around the shops, spot of lunch, and soon it's time to meet up with old Binky in his local tavern, the Quartered Wallace. It's a lovely pub," here Stewart caught Keith's glare, "but not as nice as this one, of course," he finished hurriedly.

"There was Binky, at a dark table at the back, gin ready and waiting for me. As soon as I sat down, he started talking in a scared, hurried manner. He started off by apologising, saying he wished he had told me the whole story, how I seemed like a decent chap and shouldn't be paying for another's sins. Well, this intrigued me no end, as you can imagine, and after swiftly draining his drink, he told me everything." Stewart glanced around conspiratorially, and his audience drew closer.

"Turns out, there was a lot more to the story than he first told me. Binky said he had not actually lied to me, just omitted some details. Specifically, details about the curse."

"Curse?" gasped Keith.

"That sounds a fairly major detail to omit," Ted muttered.

"I agree. So, here's the full story, as Binky heard it from Hamish, and told it to me last night, I'm telling you here now. He said when Hamish and Lulu split up, Lulu was more than angry, she was livid. Filled with Gallic rage, she was. She had powers, she told Hamish. Deep and mysterious powers from the dark forests of her homeland. Hamish scoffed at this, of course, but she went on. How had she ensnared him, caused him to love her, when no other had? Why had he picked her, a totally unsuitable French commoner, over all the Duchesses and Princesses he had been dallying with? She had used a love cipher, she told him, and if he didn't do the right thing by their child, well, it would go horribly for Hamish and his entire lineage."

"Of course, Hamish just laughed at her, but this made matters worse. She swore on her unholy gods, on her old soil, and on the blood of a cockerel, that their son would have his birthright, one way or another. Hamish told Binky she let out an unearthly scream, and said that their son would be his heir, and to make it so, she would see the old gods gave him great and terrible powers, so if he couldn't receive what was his by right legally, he could take it by force. She left then, to Hamish's relief. Binky told me that Hamish was sad over her departure for many a month, and more than once thought to try and find her, and the child that must have been delivered by now, and make it work, but the pressure of the society they were part of was too great, and he never did."

"Binky said Hamish was never quite the same again. Yeah, he laughed, and attended great society balls and functions, but it was different, almost like part of him had gone when Lulu left. Anyway, many years later, Hamish starts to get ill. Hamish knew his time was running short and he felt he had to make amends to the child he never knew and the only woman he had ever loved. Binky said it worried Hamish immensely and that it was giving him a great amount of anxiety."

"Finally, Hamish asked Binky if he could help him track down Lulu, to try and make things right before he died. Binky agreed, and after a few weeks, his investigations had a lead to a remote French village on the Belgian border, deep in the Ardennes. Binky told me that by then, my uncle's health was too poor to travel, so he wrote a letter for Lulu, begging forgiveness. If she would forgive him, it said, he would change his will and give everything to their child, and more importantly, acknowledge the child to be his son, in full, with all benefits owing."

"Binky said, of course, he would deliver the letter, await a reply, and return to Goolie as quickly as possible. He told me he set out the next day and was in Lulu's village within thirty-six hours. Binky said he knocked on the door, and the Lulu that opened it was hardly changed in over twenty years. Still a beauty, but her face had hardened, become cruel, almost. She let him in with a smile and was welcoming. She heard him out in silence, then read the letter. After reading it, Binky said, she laughed, but there was no happiness in that laugh. She crumpled up the letter and threw it in the fire. She looked Binky in the eye and said there would be no forgiveness for Hamish, his legacy was cursed and her son would take everything, will or no will."

"Binky said he tried to reason with her, but she was adamant. He went to take his leave, but as he did, she said something that hit him hard. She said that she had given the old strength to her son and he would take what was his. It was too late to stop it even if she wanted to. She had invoked the strength of the loup-garou, the werewolf. She told him the boy was out there. He can't be bargained with, he can't be reasoned with, he doesn't feel pity or remorse, or fear, and he will absolutely not stop…EVER, until he is dead."

"I miss 80s action movies," sighed Keith. Ted nodded in agreement.

"She said no forgiveness for Hamish, he would die alone and unloved. She had spent the entire life of the boy teaching him to hate poor old Hamish. Binky was crying as he told me this, great tears of sadness. He said he was enraged, angry for a friend that he loved being denied the chance to make things right on his deathbed, and he did something he was deeply sorry for. He struck Lulu, hard. She fell and dashed her brains out against the fireplace. Binky said it was unintentional and I sat there, watching this old Scottish aristocrat cry into his gin. I believed him."

"He told me when he returned, Hamish was already dead, so there was a small mercy in that he didn't have to tell a dying man his offer was rejected. I know how this all sounds, but with the bodies and Binky's story and all, I believed every word of it. Binky told me to stay away from the Hall, and I agreed that sounded the right idea. I took a room in the pub that night, and the very next morning I was on a train home. I had to change at Ashford, of course."

"Of course," agreed the others.

"And while I awaited my train, I put in a phone call to the lawyers in Goolie, instructing them to sell the house and contents forthwith. No amount of land, or fancy estates, is worth getting torn to shreds by a Lon Chaney lookalike. So, I'd rather be alive and without all that than looking over my shoulder for a bloke with a unibrow every five minutes."

The three were silent for a good few minutes, before Ted spoke up, "I see a few problems with this."

"Go on," said Stewart.

"Well, mainly, the act of selling the house doesn't stop you being the heir. You already are. The heir, I mean."

"Yeah, and what about the money? Did you give that back?" added Keith.

"Hmm. No. I see your point. But surely now, without knowing where, or indeed, who I am, the son of Lulu would have to find me, and that is a very tall order indeed."

"Not really," said a deep voice with a noticeable French accent from the fireplace. All three turned as the figure of the man in the dark coat slowly stood and turned. "What the son of a murdered mother could do is keep track of his mother's killer, disembowel him as he left the Quartered Wallace, then come back, lie in wait and follow you on your journey here."

The three friends at the bar gaped in terror, as the man drew himself to his full height. He opened his coat, removed his hat and started towards them.

"I will have what is mine, the lands and wealth, and if I cannot, I will have the blood of my father's kin on my teeth."

Keith dropped behind the bar, quaking in fear. Ted and Stewart tried to push themselves into the mahogany, clamber over the bar, anything, stools were kicked over, drinks were spilt, as the man, his shape changing as he walked towards them, his nails growing, his teeth sharpening, his face morphing, said, "Hello, cousin. By the way, this lager is shit."

"Hors d'oeuvre sir?" A posh marmot in a waiter's outfit said to Dave, as he offered him a tray of tasty looking pastries.

"Ooh, don't mind if I do," smiled Dave as he grabbed a fin full.

Dave crammed a pastry into his mouth just as an elegantly dressed earwig with a thin, waxed moustache sidled up to him.

"Hello there, old boy!" greeted the earwig cordially. "I'm Lord Isotope, pleased to meet you!" Dave smiled through his mouthful of pastry. "Now, what the devil are you?" asked Lord Isotope. Dave finally swallowed his mouthful and was just about to answer when the earwig gasped, "Why, you're a unicorn!"

Dave smiled and said, "Oh no, I'm not a unicorn, I'm a—" but he could get no further as the moustachioed Isotope interrupted him.

"A unicorn! How splendid! I see you've managed to get over that whole being mythical hurdle then?"

"No, I am not a unicorn, sorry," smiled Dave.

"Well, of course, you're a blooming unicorn! Look at you, sir!" The earwig insisted. "What on earth do you think you are then?" He bristled.

"Well, I am a narwhal," Dave said patiently.

"A narwhal?" Barked Lord Isotope incredulously, "What the deuce is a narwhal? No; you, sir, are a unicorn. I can tell by the horn."

Dave gritted his teeth, but remained polite. "No, I can quite assure you that I am a narwhal. Just like my parents before me."

"I will not be made fun of by a mythological animal!" Bellowed Isotope furiously. "Now I have no idea why you are denying that you are a unicorn, or why you are choosing to try and make a fool of me, but by criminy, I will not stand for it, sir!" He jabbed Dave in the chest with his foreleg in time with the last six syllables. He turned on his heel and strode off through the crowd.

Dave looked around. To his huge embarrassment he saw that most of the folk around him had not only heard the earwig's outburst, but were now scrutinising him with interested looks. Dave withered under their gazes and put his head down and scuttled to the nearest buffet table. He sauntered up to the sausage rolls as naturally as he could, his cheeks aflame with shame. What on earth was wrong with that earwig? He chanced a look around and was happy to see that everyone had gone back to their conversations or dance partners. Heaving a sigh of relief, he turned and faced the wonderful array of goodies laid out on the table in front of him.

Looking at all the food in front of him, Dave was suddenly happy again. He forgot all about the lunatic Lord Isotope and scooped up a flipper full of decadent looking cupcakes. He turned to face the room and bask in the loveliness of the party, popping cake after cake into his happy face. Just at that moment, he felt a tap on his shoulder. He spun to see a pair of beautiful chickens, resplendent in matching dresses of red silk. He smiled his most charming smile and said, "And what can I do for you lovely ladies?"

The chickens clucked and popped, and the one closest to him said, "Is it true?"

Dave's face fell. "Is what true?"

"Are you a unicorn?" The chicken asked. Her friend behind her stepped in.

"Of course, he's a unicorn, Esther, look at his horn!"

Dave grimaced. "I am sorry to disappoint you, ladies, but no, I am not a unicorn."

Esther cackled like only a chicken could. "Of course, you're a unicorn! Why are you trying to pull one over on Esme and me?"

Dave felt drained. "No, I am not a unicorn. I am a narwhal. Please stop this and listen to me."

Esme shrieked, "A narwhal? A naaaarwhaaaal? Whoever heard of a narwhal? You're a unicorn, my lad, and you should be proud to admit it."

Dave felt a wave of shame roll over him, as he noticed everyone nearby had stopped what they were doing to listen. For some weird reason, he started to focus in on the chicken's purses, which were indescribably tiny. *What on earth could you hold in that*, he thought. *Why bother?* Esther's horrible clucks awoke him from his reverie. "If I were a unicorn, I would be proud. I wouldn't go around pretending to be a narwhal. What's his angle, Esme?" Esme regarded Dave with a cold eye.

"It's because he's FAT!" She wittered.

All the people around them let out an audible gasp.

Dave was stunned.

"Well, look, Esther. He's fat. Everyone knows that unicorns are beautiful svelte creatures of wonder. Look at this fellow! And look!" She screamed at the top of her poultry lungs. "He's holding a cupcake!"

You could have heard a pin drop. The entire ballroom held their breath. From sticklebacks to sidewinders, all eyes were on poor Dave and the evil chicken pair.

Time stood still for Dave. Then, with a huge intake of breath, he bellowed, "WHAT! I am a NARWHAL!" He roared. "Monodon monoceros! Why won't you people let me be? And I'm not fat, I have a layer of blubber for cold temperatures."

Just at that point, trumpets burst into life. The crowd, already silent, managed to become even quieter. An overweight toad strode into the room. "Pray silence for the king!" he boomed.

All the guests dropped to their knees, even Dave in his state of shock.

Into the room strode the king. He was magnificent in yellow robes, a gorgeous, regal squirrel. His bearing made everyone gasp as he passed by them. He marched to the middle of the room, stopped, placed his hands on his hips and growled, "What the blue blazes is going on here?"

"Please, your majesty," Esme squeaked, "this unicorn is saying he isn't. A unicorn I mean. He says he's a 'narwhal'." Dave noted with horror she even did the air quotes.

"And what of it?" The king asked.

"Well, it's not right, is it?" said Esme.

Esther stood up. "No. A person should say they are what they are!" There was a murmur of agreement among the crowd.

"Dave, stand up," the king said kindly. "This is my friend Dave," he began.

"He's a damn fool," came the voice of Lord Isotope from the back of the room.

"Enough," the king said, quietly but with such squirrelly force that everyone but Dave were forced to put their eyes to the ground.

"We live in a difficult world" began the king, "and we should all do all we can to make sure each of our journeys are as easy as possible. Now this is my friend Dave. And he's a narwhal" A huge gasp ran through the crowd, "but even if he wasn't, he is a person, and he deserves the right to be called what he wants. Doesn't he?" The king surveyed the crowd, daring anyone to contradict him. But no-one did. The assembled mass slowly nodded and mumbled agreement. "So," continued the king, "let's make my friend Dave the NARWHAL welcome, shall we?"

And with that, the crowd rose and gathered around Dave, shaking his fin and patting him on the blowhole. Dave beamed with happiness as guest after guest complimented him on his horn and the oiliness of his flippers. One cheeky lady earthworm even asked him with a wink and whisper, if his butt was barnacle-free. After a few minutes, the king shouted, "strike up the band!" And the goats and gorillas played a great raucous song, as all the folk danced, and laughed, and sang. And everyone wanted to dance and laugh and sing with Dave, and he went home a very happy narwhal.

No-one noticed above the calumny and cacophony the shadowy figure of Lord Isotope lurking in the background.

"No-one makes a monkey out of Lord Isotope," he muttered furiously. "NO-ONE."

Dave the Narwhal in the Hamster Club

Dave the narwhal opened his eyes and sat up slowly in bed, a big smile across his face.

"Yes!" He shouted as he leapt from the sheets. "It's finally Tuesday!" This was aimed at his hamster, Pablo. Pablo, however, paid no attention, partly as he was used to Dave's outbursts by now, and partly because he was a hamster and couldn't understand even if he wanted to.

"Oh come on, Pablo," Dave said to his hamster, "try and be a bit excited. It's Tuesday, and that means it's the day for HAMSTER CLUB!"

Pablo eyed him with a long cool look, like only a hamster can give, then turned around and shuffled back into his bed. Dave sighed and grumbled to himself all the way to the kitchen.

"Ungrateful rodent," he muttered as he started making his breakfast, but his bad mood was gone in a trice and he was back to his usual happy self. He poured himself a bowl of his favourite cereal, Crab-O's, and sat down to enjoy his breakfast.

The best day of the month, thought Dave, *hamster club day*. He had so much to do. He had to make Pablo and his cage look respectable and do any repairs needed. Terry the woodlouse was the president of hamster club, and he was a stickler for his inspections so he had a busy morning ahead of him. Dave couldn't wait to get started, so he didn't.

Dave lifted his hamster from his cage and placed him with a careful fin into the bathtub. "Now, Pablo, I've remembered to put the plug in this time, so there's no escaping down the plughole for you today." If Pablo was upset by his chance to escape into the plumbing, he didn't show it. He scampered around in the bath, his tiny feet scritching and scratching the bath's enamel, before becoming bored of the whole thing and sitting down to watch his owner work. Dave buffed Pablo's bowl, he washed his wheel, he burnished his bars and wiped his water bottle. When all was finished, he sat on the edge of the bath and admired his work.

"It looks great!" he said to Pablo, and he gently lifted him up with a flipper. Dave peered at his pet peevishly. "Hmm, but you look scruffy, my boy. This will not do, will not do at all." He placed Pablo in the bathroom basin and gently washed him with some special shampoo he had bought from Mr Eagle, the vet. He rinsed him carefully and dried him with a fluffy towel. Dave inspected him carefully when he was done.

"You look fantastic!" Dave beamed at his friend. "Spiffing! Natty! Why, I'm sure Terry will be impressed and amazed," he continued as he lowered Pablo into his clean cage carefully. "You are sure to pass the inspection with flying colours and..." Dave felt something moist on his flipper and glanced down. "Errrr! You done a poo on me flipper, you dirty little devil!" Now, hamsters can't smile, or laugh, but as Dave rushed across to the bathroom sink and washed the small round, brown poo from his fin, you could be mistaken for thinking Pablo was giggling merrily to himself. "Yuck," Dave muttered, "it was time for my shower anyway."

And that's what he did. He showered and dressed as quickly as he could, and just as he finished, there was a ring at the doorbell. Dave scampered downstairs and opened the front door. There stood a handsome young bat. He was wearing a dark suit, and behind him was the now familiar potato-shaped car.

"Hi there, Dave, is it?" The bat stuck out a wing. Dave shook it. "I'm Alastair, Alastair the bat. I'm your—"

"Aha! My tuber driver! Perfect!" Dave interrupted, a little rudely. Alastair the bat didn't mind though as he was an easy-going bat. Dave ran back inside the house, grabbed Pablo's cage, trotted to the idling car and climbed in next to the waiting Alastair.

"Hamster club HQ, is it, guv?" Asked the bat.

"Please!" Answered Dave cheerfully.

"I'll get you there in ten minutes!" Said Alastair. And he did.

Dave walked the few paces down Terry's pathway carrying Pablo in his cage and rang the bell. The door was opened by Sheila the woodlouse, Terry's wife.

"Hi Dave. Hi Pablo!" She smiled happily as she waved them in. "Come on through to the living room, Terry is just about to start."

Dave didn't really approve of Sheila referring to hamster club HQ as her living room, but he was a polite narwhal on the whole and didn't complain as he followed her down the hallway.

"Dave's here!" She announced as she opened the living room door. Dave could see all the members of the hamster club were there and greeted his friends as he entered the room. There was Todd the Macaw and his hamster Chappie. There was Margot the Gazelle and her hamster Lady. Next to her on the sofa was her friend Suzie the Vole and her hamster Fluffy. Last but certainly not least, there stood Terry, president of the hamster club, his hamster Sir Norman Foster studying the room with a wary eye from his cage on the coffee table. Dave plopped Pablo's cage onto the coffee table alongside the others and sat down.

"Ah, good to see such a great turnout for hamster club." Terry smiled.

"Well, I will let you get on now," smiled Sheila as she blew her husband a kiss. "I've made some lemonade, it's over there," she pointed with one of her many legs and smiled at the group as she shut the door.

"Thank you all for attending this month's meeting of hamster club," Terry smiled at his guests. "Today is a bit of a special day, and I have an announcement to make before I do the inspection." A hush filled the room, as all eyes fell on him. "Sheila and I have been doing some thinking, and we have decided that—oh bother!" The doorbell chimed loudly from the hallway. "Now who the blooming flip is that? Oh well, Sheila will get it." He took a sip of his lemonade and continued. "As I was saying—" All eyes turned to the door as it opened a fraction and Sheila's face peered around.

"Sorry to disturb you all," she smiled happily, "but you've got a new member!"

"Well, bring them in!" Terry shouted welcomingly. The other members of the hamster club looked at each other with excited faces. They had not had a new member in years! They all leant forwards as Sheila stepped out of the doorway and was replaced by...

"Lord Isotope, at yer service." Beamed the aristocratic earwig as he entered the room. Dave gasped as the other members of his club all rose from their seats and fussed around the earwig, making him welcome. Finally, Lord Isotope made his way over to the armchair which contained Dave. He held out a leg to him and, with a nasty look in his eye, he said, "Lord Isotope. Pleased to meet you."

"Dave," said Dave, and offered him a flipper. "But we've already met."

"Have we, by Jove? Well, I don't remember that. I'm sure I would have remembered meeting a unicorn." He smiled nastily.

Dave's face fell. His mouth flapped open and shut.

"Oh, he's not a unicorn, Lord Isotope. He's a narwhal," said Margot.

"A narwhal, eh?" Said the earwig. "Well, pleased to meet you, Darren, was it?"

"Dave," said Dave again. "As well you know," he added under his breath.

Terry eventually quietened down the chatter and called the meeting to order.

"Well, this is an extraordinary meeting of the hamster club for many reasons now." Terry smiled at the room.

"Why are you here?" Dave whispered in the ear of Isotope.

The earwig didn't take his eyes off Terry as he hissed back, "Had a feller look into you, Dave my boy, after you humiliated me in front of the king." Dave started to protest but Isotope spoke over him, "Seems that you like this stupid hamster club almost as much as I used to like being in the king's court. I say used to, of course, can't go back now, not after the embarrassment you caused me." Dave looked horrified.

"I did no such thing!" He whispered frantically. "You insulted me and insisted I was a unicorn! And those chickens didn't help!" Dave looked up and realised Terry had finished talking and everyone was looking at him.

"All okay?" Terry asked Dave. "Good. Then I will carry on. As I was saying, Sheila and I have decided, that after all these years as the president of the hamster club, it's time for me to step aside and let someone else take charge."

"WHAT?" Chorused the hamster club.

"Yep, I've been at the helm nearly twenty years now, which is remarkable, if only for the fact woodlice usually only live two. I need to slow down, spend time with Sheila. So, effective immediately, I will tender my resignation. Now, I have thought long and hard about this and as my last act as president, I would like to nominate Margot to fill my shoes. She has been most valuable to me these last few years in her role as secretary and I think she would do a great job." And Terry sat down.

Margot stood up and smiled nervously.

"Well, this is a surprise," she started. "Thank you, Terry, and I think I speak for all of us when I say thank you for all your hard work as the president of hamster club." Terry smiled as she continued, "As your new president, I hope to continue—"

"Hold on. Hold on, I say," Lord Isotope interrupted. "But aren't we supposed to vote on the president?"

"Well, yes," chimed in Todd the macaw, "but you heard Terry, he wants Margot to succeed him, and she'd do a great job, and no-one else is standing, so…" He tailed off.

"Why, my good fellow, I fully intend to run for president myself," barked the earwig.

A hush ran around the room. Todd looked at Margot. Margot looked at Suzie. Suzie looked at Terry. Terry looked at Isotope. Dave looked sick. Pablo looked for a seed.

"Oh. Okay, if Lord Isotope here, our newest member at his first meeting, wants to challenge Margot, a member in fine standing for many years, we should put it to a vote," said Terry. "All those in favour of Margot, raise a—"

"Wait, wait," said Isotope, rising up from the chair. "Shouldn't we have a debate first?".

"Yes, I suppose so," sighed Terry. "The debate will start in five minutes."

Everyone milled around chatting to Margot. All except for Dave, who cornered Isotope. "What the bloody hell are you doing, Isotope?" The unpleasant earwig smiled.

"Getting my revenge on you, my boy. It's happened much more quickly than I had hoped, but now I can become president of this stupid little club and make your life miserable."

Dave was horrified. "What? You can't do that? I love hamster club!"

"I know." Isotope chuckled horribly.

"Order, order," called Terry. "Okay. let's get this show on the road. I suggest we make this a chat between the candidates, and after they've both finished, we hold the vote. Agreed?"

"Agreed," chorused the hamster club.

"Okay, Margot, would you like to start?"

"Thank you, Mr President." Margot rose nervously to her feet. "As most of you know, I have been a member here for many years, since my first hamster Missy, and after her Wendy, and now my beloved Lady. I have attended all meetings, and I think worked hard. I would like to carry on the work that you have started, Terry." A smattering of applause here. "Thank you, I think that about covers it."

"Does it? Does it indeed, Miss Gazelle?" said Isotope, rising from his chair. "Hey guys, friends, my fellow hamster owners. Aren't you sick of the way this club is being run?" He looked around the room into the shocked eyes of the other animals. "The current administration has run this once noble club into the ground." The other animals looked shocked and confused. "The other hamster clubs laugh at us. Laugh. Everybody says so, okay?"

"Now hold on just a minute," Terry sputtered in outrage.

"No, sir, you hold on," countered Isotope. "This is my time to speak. As I said, we have become a laughingstock amongst all the other hamster clubs in the kingdom. A laughingstock!"

Todd raised his hand. "I thought we were the only hamster club in the kingdom?"

"That's fake news!" shrieked Isotope. "There are hundreds of other hamster clubs here, you are just too stupid to realise it. And every single one is laughing at us. Laughing. Only I, with my awesome brain and huge wealth, can make hamster club great again."

Dave looked around the room. Terry looked horrified, Margot shocked. Suzie was flicking through her copy of the club rules. Todd looked thoughtful. "Really?" said Todd. "Why are they laughing at us?"

"Because your current administration is a joke," Isotope snarled. "This low-energy woodlouse and his gazelle minion are the elite, they are your enemy," Isotope glared around the room before continuing, "As your president, I promise that all hamsters will have upgraded cages, and as much of whatever it is they like to eat as they want! I promise a new dawn and it's going to be beautiful."

Dave stood up. "But Margot here has kept hamsters for years. She's one of us, a friend." Margot smiled at Dave gratefully. "This is your first day at hamster club. Why should we listen to you? You don't know the first thing about hamsters."

"Maybe I don't," snarled Isotope. "But I am rich. Amazingly, fabulously rich. And that, in my mind, qualifies me for any job."

Todd spoke up, "Actually, that makes sense, Dave, when you think about it. And maybe it is time for a change? These two have been in charge a long time now, maybe it's time for someone else's ideas."

"What?" said Dave. "That makes no sense at all. Just because he's rich doesn't mean he knows the first thing about hamsters or their clubs."

"This is an outrage." Margot shook with rage. "There are no other hamster clubs, no-one is laughing at us."

"Fake news!" screamed Isotope.

"Look," Margot continued, "you've known me years. You were there, Todd, for me, when I lost Missy and Wendy."

"And how, pray tell, did we lose those two beautiful hamsters, Misty and Windy?" Smirked Isotope.

"Missy and Wendy, you mean?" Margot corrected him, as tears started to spring to her eyes. "Well, they both got very old, and eventually they died." She sobbed.

"Oh did they?" asked Isotope. "Was there an investigation?"

"Well, no," cried Margot. "I buried them in the back garden."

"AHA!" crowed the earwig. "Hiding the evidence? Disposing of the bodies before a proper investigation? I put it to you, my friends here, that Margot murdered her hamsters and covered it up!" A gasp came from everyone.

Terry responded angrily, "That's outrageous! You can't just lie like that! Margot is good and kind and has never killed any hamsters." Turning to the crying gazelle, he asked quietly, "have you?"

"Of course not!" She cried with a wail.

"This tragedy has gone on far too long. Only I can make hamster club great again," barked Isotope. "Let's put it to the vote now. How say you?"

"WAIT!" Shouted Dave. "WAIT!" All eyes turned to him. "He doesn't even have a hamster!"

They all gasped and looked at the coffee table. It was true. There was Lady, and Chappie, and Pablo, and Sir Norman Foster, but Isotope had not brought a hamster.

"Erm, yes I do," said Isotope, but he looked worried. "It's at home in my beautiful mansion. In a gold cage. Lots of people say so."

"You can't be in the hamster club without a hamster," Dave said triumphantly. He looked towards Suzie who looked up and smiled in confirmation.

"Dave's right," she said. "It's rule number two, in fact. Right after don't talk about hamster club. No-one can become a member without a hamster."

"But...I do have one," Isotope burbled, "it's at home."

"Rule three," continued Suzie, "members must bring their hamster to hamster club, or risk expulsion."

Dave leapt to his feet and shouted, "I vote to expel Lord Isotope for not bringing his hamster to his first ever meeting."

"Seconded!" Beamed Margot.

"No, wait, I'm rich you see, so you should listen to me, I'm so much better than you normal animals..." Isotope started to babble.

Terry pretended not to hear him. "All those in favour of expelling Lord Isotope due to hamster-based infractions?"

"Aye," shouted everyone but Isotope.

"Oh you fools, you poor, stupid fools!" Raged Isotope as he started towards the door. "This is not the last you will hear of this, mark my words! I'm rich, I have the biggest and bestest brain, I demand you put me in charge so I can pick on the narwhal!" But no-one listened.

"Motion carried," shouted Terry over the enraged earwig. "Please leave, Lord Isotope."

And he did, but not without shouting and threatening and even shamefully crying and begging to be allowed to boss them all about, but it fell on deaf ears.

And after he left, the remaining members of the hamster club breathed a sigh of relief and celebrated with new president Margot.

And at the end of the day, Dave went home, climbed into bed and smiled a little smile just before he fell asleep.

Hamster club had always been great, he thought before falling asleep.

But Isotope wasn't done, not by a long chalk, as Dave would soon find out.

Pramface

I had only been residing with my Nan for a few months when I first saw the girl with the pram. At the time, I sat on a wall by the all-night garage awaiting Anton, as usual. He was inside the garage trying to convince the new girl that he was old enough to buy some fags. I had elected to wait outside, partly to help shield his embarrassment when he failed on his eternally doomed mission, partly because it was actually quite clement a day for once and I didn't want to waste the sunshine.

Then, I saw her walking towards me on the other side of the road, pushing her pram, and didn't pay too much attention at first. The estate was full of young girls pushing prams, it was our only growth industry. I turned my attention to Anton and watched his struggled attempts at getting served through the window of the garage, his body language a silent pantomime of outraged bargaining. With a smile, I shook my head and could see the girl had drawn closer to me, close enough to see her fully for the first time. She was dressed, as all of us on the estate were, I suppose, like a poor person. Shabby off-brand trainers, three-stripe joggers worn at the cuff, an oversized non-descript hoodie. She had almost the perfect uniform of all females from the area aged between ten and thirty, but she sported a noticeable exception—a large, heavy quilt wrapped around her shoulders, large enough to extend into the pram to form a blanket, affixed to the hood with mismatched clothes' pegs to give the child within some much needed warmth, darkness and privacy. The blanket was large and bulky, certainly requisitioned from a bed somewhere.

This practice was not uncommon then, as winter coats were expensive and fitted pram blankets were an unaffordable luxury. The pram itself was a superannuated model, held together more by tape and the occupant's prayers than by any sort of structural integrity. I noted the handle had snapped at some point in the past, and the two remaining posts had been crudely taped, to prevent cuts to the hands of those that would push it, I supposed. The frame sagged and creaked in an alarming manner, and the body, where the baby lay, was bulged and stained. All in all, not much different from the legions of prams pushed by all the legions of girls in that part of the world.

The girl herself, however, was noticeably different. She was short and not much older than I, if at all. Her hair was thin and had been bleached to the colour and texture of straw, but a good four inches of dark roots betrayed its natural colour. It hung to her shoulders, loose and uncared for. Her eyes were fixed on the pavement in front of the pram, but as she approached she looked at me briefly before flicking her gaze away, almost nervously. Her face was plain, pinched cheeks, a small pointed nose. Her skin was sallow, and she looked drained, almost painfully so. Again, no different to any of the countless other girls I saw every day.

It was the look her face held that made her different, a look of colossal sadness and heartbreak that I had only witnessed once before: in the mirror. She had the same look in her eyes that I had seen in my own every day since my mum had been placed in the hospital and I had come to live with my Nan. I instantly felt some kinship with the girl and flashed her a brief smile which she didn't see as she bustled past me. I watched her as she continued down the narrow street, the pram grunting in protest at every crack and rut in the paving slabs, until she rounded a corner and was gone from my sight. I turned my attention back to the garage, and was surprised to see Anton strutting towards me, an air of victory surrounding him.

The second he knew he had my attention, he stopped dead in the middle of the garage forecourt, spread his legs wide and thrust a fist containing a small gold cardboard box above his head.

"Toldja she'd serve me, bruv!" He shouted in triumph.

"F*ckin' 'ell, Anton, how the f*ck didja manage to pull that one off?" I asked in genuine amazement.

Anton was sixteen, but looked much younger due to his slim frame and ratty visage. He was dressed like me, like all the boys in the area, adopting the appearance of the rest of the herd so no-one stood out as a target for the older, more brutal males. His mother was well known as an accommodating lady, fond of a party and the company of men. It was during one of these parties, when Anton was an infant, that one of his mother's male companions had taken umbrage to the baby's cries for attention and had twisted the child's arm viciously behind its back, in a failed attempt to quieten him. His mother had been passed out on the sofa at the time, and when she arose the next day, Anton's cries had subdued to a keening whimper. His arm was a shade of purple by then, and his mother, not wishing the attention of child protection services, had elected to forgo the hospital trip and treat him herself.

As a result, Anton's left arm was twisted, useless and hung permanently by his side. Anton had never known the name of his father, or the man that had crippled him for life, and his mother had long forgotten. Despite his physical shortcomings, however, Anton was blessed with an easy smile and a quick wit. At the time, he was my only friend on the estate; as we know, the tide of fate sometimes drives the flotsam together.

"F*ckin' easy, toldja it would be." Anton grinned as he danced towards me happily. "Just gave the b*tch a bit of the old Ant-man magic, she was all over me. I reckon I could have a go on her if I wanted." I glanced towards the garage window at this, and thought the likelihood of a thirty-something woman wanting to risk jail time as a sex offender for sleeping with the underage Anton to be a touch far-fetched. I thought it prudent to hold my counsel. Anton did have the cigarettes, after all.

Months passed, and I fell more in step with the others on the estate. My Nan clothed and fed me, nothing more. There was no kindness, only obligation, and I missed my mother terribly.

I had not seen her since the day she had been admitted. Every attempt at broaching the subject with Nan was met with an angry explanation of our current finances which already had a considerable strain by my very existence. There was no money for the bus fare. There were no stamps so I could write, and even if there were, I did not know the name of the hospital in which she resided. Phone calls were equally out of the question, so I resigned myself to my new life. Anton made it easier, and within time our circle expanded to include a trio of young ladies who were equally on the periphery of estate society.

Cindy, Courtnee and Lee-an were all related, and lived together in the same house under the supposed watchful eye of Big Nick, the father of Cindy and Lee-an. Courtnee was a cousin to the girls, and had lived with them for a number of years. She was a dull, lumpen, bovine creature, and it was she I had been courting the last few weeks. Her breath smelt continually of cigarettes, and her flesh of fried food. Her womanhood tasted strangely of gherkins. There was no desire from me in our brief frenzied rutting, sometimes privately in my Nan's living room when she was at the bingo or the local pub, occasionally with the other three looking dispassionately on if the mood swept us while we were al fresco.

Truth be told, the only emotion I had towards Courtnee was indifference, our coupling born mainly out of boredom, peer pressure, and the fact it was marginally more pleasurable than self-manipulation. I was beginning to fear, however, that pregnancy could play a real part in our future, as Courtnee despised the use of prophylactics. She was fourteen, and I fifteen, both too young, I felt, to be avoiding the responsibilities of parenthood. Sadly, however, it appeared that she had deemed me something of a catch, and her primitive attempts at seduction were becoming more urgent, afraid as she was that I would move on to fresher fields before I had planted my seed. The strain of the differing expectations on the relationship was starting to show, and an already mundane partnership was becoming frayed.

On my part, my indifference had turned swiftly from barely tolerance to actual avoidance. Courtnee, on the other hand, had seen the relationship start to slip away and had responded with a possessiveness that had escalated over the last few weeks, becoming increasingly confrontational and violent.

She had taken to following me at a distance, or sending her cousins to do the same, convinced as she was of my infidelities. I was not pursuing any other girls, I was simply bored with her, but how could I explain that? Courtnee's temper had flared on more than one occasion, culminating in her threatening a number of other neighbourhood girls with violence if they so much as talked to me. I didn't care too much about that, to be honest, I was more shocked than anything at the transformation from passive ruminant to hot-headed scrapper. This had hurried my agenda, and at the time I was eagerly seeking a way out of the courtship while still maintaining the lady's honour and public standing. This all came to head on a day that I saw the girl with the pram once more. Don't misunderstand, I had seen her many times since the first, but always from afar. This occasion, however, a Saturday in late September, would prove itself to be quite fateful.

The day started regularly enough. I awoke at ten, my usual hour at the weekend. The previous evening, Anton had purloined a bottle of his mother's latest paramours' vodka, and he and I had imbibed freely in my Nan's kitchen. I struggled to sit upright in my bed, my head pounding and nausea roiling around my innards. A few minutes was all it took to clear, fortunately, and I soon felt well enough to descend into the kitchen in search of some form of sustenance.

My Nan was absent, had not returned that night by all appearances. This was in no way unusual, Friday nights had become noticeably more festive over the last few weeks, and her return on Saturday lunchtime smelling of pubs and sex was inevitable and commonplace. Her socialising had become more virulent and passionate recently, due in no small part to the reality of her impending forty-fifth birthday.

As I awaited the kettle's whistle, I gave myself a brief once over. I was in dire need of some fresh clothes, but the elephantine mound of unwashed laundry piled on the kitchen table told me I was out of luck on that front. I took an exploratory sniff of my armpits and decided that a quick blast of lynx Africa would suffice for the day's events. I attended to my toilette, drank my cup of tea and headed out to see what the day would hold.

I strolled in good spirits to what we optimistically called the green. In reality, a more truthful moniker would have been 'the yellow' because so badly had the grass there been choked with litter and dog sh*t. It was a fairly large area situated about half a mile from my Nan's. While the original planners had in mind a lush, verdant area for recreation and exercise, the reality was very different. Half the space was taken up by two unmarked football pitches, which miraculously still had intact goalposts. The grass, however, was sallow and cut infrequently. This, coupled with the quite astonishing amounts of faeces that lay strewn over the surface, swiftly turned any attempts at playing into a depressing experience.

There was a small, melancholy playground at the far end, which consisted of a swing set that had once supported four swings. Sadly, now only one remained in working order, two being terminally entangled at the apex of the A frame and one missing entirely. A small climbing frame with a slide attached crouched miserably amongst broken beer bottles, and a wooden roundabout missing both slats and purpose completed the group. A huddle of unwell looking trees made up the last part of the green, and it was these trees that had borne witness to most, if not all, of mine and Courtnee's fresh air unions.

As with all places in communal use, a swift hierarchy had formed. The apex children had the run of the place, of course, but mainly chose to stick to the wooded area, the foliage offering privacy from prying eyes for their various nefarious practices. The smaller, weaker children usually grouped at the playground, which left the football pitches to chaps like Anton and me—too large to be in the playground, too unpopular to be admitted into the woods. Obviously, these rules were unspoken and fluid, so often, a small, unliked child could find himself alone and spend a few happy minutes investigating the tree area, before someone further up the food chain arrived and chased them off, often with violence.

Upon my arrival, I was pleased to see that the autumnal drizzle and the relative earliness of the hour meant that I was the only person there, and I quickly took residence in the copse of trees. I occupied myself happily for a few minutes by poking around the detritus, checking all beer cans and bottles for any remains (there were none) and looking for any discarded cigarette butts that may still be serviceable. It was in this quest I was successful, as to my joy I found nearly half of a Lambert and Butler, nestled within a tree root miraculously untouched by the damp that was falling now more steadily from the heavens. This I lit with a disposable lighter retrieved from the depths of my trackie bottoms, and a wave of pleasure washed over me as I inhaled the acrid smoke.

Presently, a few minutes passed, and from across the football pitch I espied a figure limping towards the bench that sat at what would have been the halfway line. After a second, I recognised it to be Anton, and extinguishing my cigarette with my heel, I walked from the trees towards him. He reached the bench and slumped onto it, and as I approached the limp was explained. Anton was beaten black and blue. He nodded to me in acknowledgement as I sat next to him, puzzlement and no small amount of horror on my face. "What the fuck happened?" I asked.

"That f*cking c*nt Welsh Billy beat the f*cking sh*t out of me. He missed the bottle of voddy straight away and knocked the crap out of me as soon as I got in from yours," Anton grunted from between split lips.

His right eye was closed and already the colours of oil on water. Two dried rivulets of blood ran between his nostrils and his mouth, and I could see blood had dried and caked around the opening to his ear canal. "F*ck Anton, you okay?" I asked, real worry in my voice.

"No. No, I'm f*cking not!" gasped Anton, and then the unthinkable happened, he began to sob.

"I'm f*cking sick of all the loser c*nts that are always at my house using me as a f*cking punching bag, I'm sick of my c*nt of a b*tch mother letting them." His head fell to his chest and he started letting out huge racking sobs. "One day, one day, my dad will come and find me, and he will make them all pay, my c*nting mother, Welsh f*cking Billy, and especially the c*nt that gave me this." At this, he swung his body sharply at the hip, his crippled arm swinging in front of him, lifeless. "All of them. My dad was a boxer and he will beat the f*cking shit out of all of them c*nts," he snarled, teeth bared like an animal.

I knew his fantasy of old. Anton and his mother both had no idea who his father was, it could conceivably even be Welsh Billy. The dream of being rescued by his father was just that, a dream. He slumped back on the bench, chest hitching in soundless sobs. I wished he would stop. If a larger child were to see him, it would end badly, with another beating or worse. A minute or two passed and mercifully he pulled himself together. Wiping his face with the sleeve of his hoodie, Anton looked at me.

"So d' ya know what I did, bruv?" he asked me, and I could see a familiar spark of mischief in him.

"What did you f*cking do?" I asked, eager to hear of my friend's vengeance.

"I only went and f*cking nicked this c*nt off him, din' I?" Anton smiled, and unzipped his tracksuit top with a wince of pain. From inside, he pulled out a half full bottle of Jose Cuervo tequila. The clear liquid sloshed inside with an oily sheen. I marvelled at my friend's foolhardy heroism.

"Oh you f*cking muppet, he will f*cking do you for sure when he finds out!" I laughed at his audacity. "He will f*cking kill you."

Anton shrugged. "I don't really care anymore, bruv," he said quietly, almost to himself, and I believed him. Anton unscrewed the cap and took a long pull of the liquor. He let out an involuntary shudder as he handed it to me. "F*ck me, that's smooth," he retched. "No wonder that Welsh tw*t likes it so much." He looked at me. "You not having any, pussy? You making me drink alone? Thought we was tight."

"F*ck alright," I said with feigned exasperation and took a swig. Instantly, the burn in my trachea made me cough and splutter uncontrollably, and my face pulled itself into a ghastly rictus. "Sh*t 'Ton, you're right, that's f*cking spot on," I lied.

We sat in silence, we two, on that bench for a while, the bottle passing between us both. The drizzle did not worry us unduly, but we both pulled our hoods over our heads to offer some degree of defence. My thoughts had drifted towards my problem with Courtnee when I was roused from my reverie by "You won't, you know, f*cking tell anyone I cried, will you?" He asked, his eyes straight ahead, not meeting mine.

"No, 'course not, you bell-end," I replied, touched by his vulnerability.

"Thanks, mate," he sniffed and turned to me, "things are already hard enough for me around here with this," he gestured to his withered arm, "without any of those sharky c*nts thinking I'm some kind of crying ponce."

I had no answer for that, so I kept my own counsel. I started to wish I had funds for cigarettes, and was about to suggest going back to my place to see if I could pilfer any from my Nan, when the girl with the pram hove into view. She stood hesitantly on the edge of the park, her eyes flicking quickly over the area, the eyes of the prey watching out for predators.

Apparently and unsurprisingly, Anton and I didn't register as a threat to her, because tentatively she stepped onto the grass. Today she was dressed not dissimilarly from the previous times I had seen her, and the ubiquitous blanket was there, pegged to the pram hood. Anton had not registered her presence and was silent, lost in revenge fantasies, I imagined.

I tracked her path as she circumnavigated the pitch, her eyes never straying from the path in front of her, neither acknowledging the damp in the air nor her child in the pram.

Presently, she turned a corner, and her progress would bring her inexorably towards our bench unless she deviated for some reason. I looked towards her as she approached and saw that sad, drained desperation I saw in myself, and today, in Anton. I resolved to speak to her, for if she were as lost as we, surely some contact would lighten her load. I saw her catch my eyes, but she immediately looked to the floor, the submissive gesture of all victims in this infernal jungle.

This time, I refused to look away, and a few steps later, she looked up and met my gaze. This time she let it linger for a second, puzzlement furrowing her brow, unsure as to my intent. I saw her wariness and gave her a small half smile of encouragement. She instantly looked at the floor again, but this time the faintest hint of a smile played across her lips.

"Who the f*ck is that chick? You know her?" Anton asked, obviously returned from his dreamworld of horrific vengeance.

"Nah man, I seen her about, you know?" I answered. She was a good few metres away and still out of earshot, but not for long.

"You looking to tap that?" He asked, his eyes flicking over her, appraising her as she approached.

"Nah man, well, I dunno, I just think she looks alone. Like us."

Anton grunted, pursed his lips, then shrugged at this. "Fair enough. You mind if I try and bang it?"

I laughed aloud at this. "Sure man, you can try if you want, big dog. She's gonna shoot you down though."

"F*ck nah man, I'm the Ant-man, I got skills," he laughed. She was a few steps from us now, and she had slowed her pace. She was watching us with amusement and wariness, our laughter seemingly alien to her. I realised I had no plan, no way with my limited social skills to open a conversation with this strange girl, and I truly believe she would have passed me by that day if it was not for Anton.

"Hey girl," he leered, his slumped posture immediately turning into confidence. I noticed he turned his body slightly, his withered arm slightly hidden by the movement. "You from the estate?"

She stopped dead and regarded us with unsteady eyes, trying to weigh up whether we were friend or foe. Anton spotted her unsurety and laughed, turning his body the other direction, angling his disabled arm towards her in plain sight. "Sh*t love, I can't hurt you, not with this gimpy wing." He nodded towards me. "And my main man here, he's such a pussy he couldn't hurt a rat." She smiled at this, a real smile, and some of the darkness fled from her face. I realised that in another place, another time, she would be half the way to attractive.

"Yeah, I'm from here," she replied, a thin, reedy voice that almost creaked with rustiness. "You get hit by a bus?" she asked.

Anton smiled, causing him to wince in pain from his split lips. "Nah, you know that c*nt Welsh Billy?" He asked. Her face was devoid of recognition. "Well, him, anyway, he done me good for nicking his vodka while he banged me Mum."

The girl looked sad at this. "I dunt really know anyone here. We only moved here a couple of years ago. I'm not really good at making friends." As she answered Anton, I saw her eyes flick to me, then cast downwards shyly. Her hands remained clenched on the taped handles of the pram. "He f*ckin' did a number on your mug though, dint'ee?"

"Yeah, that's why I nicked this off the c*nt," laughed Anton as he tilted the bottle of tequila towards her. "You dry, love?"

She laughed then, and while it certainly was not the prettiest laugh I had ever heard, or the most humour-filled—in fact, it was like her voice, thin, weak and unused—it was a laugh that I would never forget. "You're f*cking mental, you." She pushed the pram closer until she was directly in front of us. Cautiously, she pried a hand from the pram and accepted the bottle. She wiped the rim with her sleeve, a gesture strangely both charming and inoffensive. The girl partook of a deep draught, and to her credit there was no shudder, like with Anton and me. She handed the bottle to me, and I hoped to think her gaze stayed on me a little longer, just for a fraction of time, but nevertheless.

I took the bottle gratefully, and this time tried my hardest to disguise the shiver. Feeling the attention of the other two on me, I felt the urge to break the silence as I passed the bottle back to Anton.

"So, what, it's just you and the sprog?" I gestured towards the silent, covered pram.

"Oh. Well. Yeah. Just me and Kaylee, yeah. Just us two. I'm Kylie, by the way."

"Kaylee and Kylie? Niiiice!" Anton laughed, taking a drink and passing the bottle to Kylie. "The dad not around?"

"No. Kaylee's dad isn't in the picture," she answered, a little sadness creeping back into her voice. She was pressed up tight to the body of the pram, and now, for the first time, there was a hint of a stir from the depths. A tiny, wheezy cry started up from beneath the blanket. Instantly, Kylie handed the bottle to me and started to jig the handles while making soothing coos.

"F*ck me, love, if you need to breastfeed the kid, we don't mind, eh bruv?" Giggled Anton. "Just whack 'em out, we can give you our honest opinion, yeah?"

"F*ck off," snarled Kylie, but there was mischief in her faux anger, she was smiling. "Think I'd let a couple of tossers like you have a look at these beauts?" She arched her back at this. "Anyway, Kaylee isn't breastfed." This, with an air of seriousness.

"Got any fags?" I asked, more for a want of having my voice heard than any desire for a cigarette.

"Nah man, they's for mugs. Don't touch 'em. I'll take a puff though if either you two w*nkers are holding?" Kylie asked hopefully. Kaylee had ceased her fussing and a soft, contented snore could be heard emanating from beneath the blanket. Sadly, I had not had the money for any weed in weeks, and Anton had been dry for about as long himself. We conveyed the sad news, which Kylie took with good spirits.

The tequila was beginning to take hold and, not wishing to lose face with my friends, I pressed the bottle to my closed lips and pretended to take a slug. I passed the bottle quickly to Anton, who nestled it in the fork of his crotch. The drizzle had relented and I lowered my hood as Kylie started to unconsciously brush droplets of moisture from the blanket that protected her and her child. "You know, you're the first people who have tried to talk to me in yonks," said Kylie, her eyes fixed on the hood of the pram. "I really can't remember the last time I spoke for this much. Except for chatting to Kaylee, of course."

"It can be tough here, 'specially if you don't know anyone. Why don't you and Kaylee hang out with us every now and then? We don't do much but you're welcome to do it with us," I added as nonchalantly as possible. I didn't dare watch her reaction, but when I did pluck up the courage to glance at her, it was to witness an astonishing change. A smile, huge and genuine, had transformed her face. Gone was the haunted sallowness, chased away like shadows by the midday sun. It was replaced by a look of happiness and acceptance that I don't think I had ever seen before, or since. A warmth came from inside of me, too, the warmth of holding out a hand of friendship to one as alone as Anton and I. It felt good.

Kylie looked shyly at the floor, then at Anton and me, and, with what looked like tears starting to form in her eyes began to speak slowly. "Oh, thanks, that would be really nice. I, that is we, have been so lonely since we moved here…"

"Who the F*CK do you fink you're talking to, you f*cking pramface slag?" Courtnee came roaring across the football pitch, red-faced with proprietorial rage. She was orbited by her cousins, Cindy and Lee-an, both of whom had ugly sneers on their ugly faces.

Kylie's eyes widened in shock and her hands gripped the pram so tightly I feared she would snap what was left of the handles clean off. By the time Anton and I struggled to our feet, the three had already closed the distance, Courtnee in the vanguard spitting expletives so vehemently that her cigarette fell from her lips and was crushed underfoot in her rush to confront Kylie. Kylie shrank into herself and moved protectively over the pram, turning her back to Courtnee slightly to shield the child within from her jealous rage.

"What the f*ck is going on here, eh?" Screamed Courtnee, and anger seemed to make her grow in stature.

Anton realised the danger and moved quicker than I, to my eternal shame. He swiftly placed the bottle on the ground and sprang up. Effortlessly, he slid into the diminishing space betwixt Courtnee and Kylie, holding his good hand out in a placating manner. "Hey, hey, woah, slow down, Courtnee, ain't nuffink going down, we was just chatting, alright?"

"Just chattin'? Just chattin'? I'll give you just chattin', you f*cking gimpy armed little tw*t." And with that Courtnee slammed her fist into Anton's temple, hard. He went down instantly, as if the bones had been removed from his legs. I am no medical professional, but I could see, even with my youthful inexperience, that Anton had been hurt badly. Courtnee did not flinch, she stepped over Anton's form and began pushing Kylie on the shoulder. "What the f*ck do you have to say for yourself, you f*cking slag? You wanna f*ck my boyfriend, is that it?"

Kylie shrank from every push, and made to push forward, but her way was blocked by Cindy and Lee-an. Refusing to remove her hands from the pram, she turned around, fear in her eyes, and addressed Courtnee, "No, no, it's not like that, we was just talking—"

I managed to reclaim my wits and grabbed Courtnee from behind. I twisted her roughly by her shoulders so she was facing me, her back now to Kylie.

"Look, f*cking calm it, willya?" I near-screamed in her face. "There's nuffink going on. We was just talking shit, ya know? Just f*cking banter."

"I'm not f*cking avvin' it, you talking to a f*cking slag like that!" she screamed back at me, her face purple and apoplectic with rage. Spit flew from her mouth and showered my face. It was an unpleasant experience.

"Oh f*ck off then, you crazy b*tch," I snarled at her, angry now. I think also some part of my brain had registered that Anton had not got up yet, in fact, wasn't moving at all. I pushed her with both hands to the chest, hard. She fell to the ground with a thump. She looked at me with anger so pure I thought she might explode with rage, but beneath that, I saw she was actually hurt, actually felt betrayed. I was so surprised that I actually felt sorry for her, that I saw her, however briefly, as a person with feelings and hopes. It didn't last long.

"Fine, fine! You're welcome to each other," she scrambled to her feet, the anger now being replaced with pain. "You f*cking have 'im, you f*cking homewrecker slag. I don't want him." Her eyes had started to glass up as she backed away. "Only thing that limp d*ck could do is bring up anuvver man's kid, he couldn't get hard enough to get me pregnant, the limp d*ck maggot d*ck W*NKER." With that, she turned on her heel and stormed off, the sounds of her sobs evident to us all.

Relief washed over me instantly. That Courtnee had only hit one of us and had taken it upon herself to end our courtship was a fine result for me. The feeling of consolation only lasted for a second however. I turned to comfort Kylie and saw the faces of the sisters, Cindy and Lee-an. Their countenances, usually so dull and vacant, were now both fixed in a grin both malicious and calculating. I saw they had both gripped the pram during my conversation with their cousin. The colour had almost totally drained from Kylie and I saw her mouth flapping open and shut with the horror of precognition.

"I hope you can run fast, pramface," Cindy sneered. In unison, the sisters braced their feet and ripped the pram from Kylie's grasp, intending for it to speed across the grass, at no small risk to Kaylee. I leapt forward to catch the pram, but alas, I fell short and landed face first in the mud. Kylie, who weighed about as much as half of one sister alone, was no match for their flabby vindictiveness. She let out a scream of such blood-curdling horror that I hear it still, even now, on the darkest of nights.

I turned to look from my place on the ground. The pram had shot off at a great rate of knots. The force of the shove had torn the blanket from around Kylie, and it trailed behind the pram like a banner. What it revealed left the three of us, the sisters and I, in a state of paralysed horror. There was a very good reason we never saw Kylie without Kaylee, now the blanket had been forcibly removed, we could see that now.

The blanket had covered a hole that she had cut in her hoodie. Attached to her stomach was a terrible milky-skinned form. Her legs (for despite the malformation, one could plainly see that the poor creature was female) had withered to the size of a child's arm and they straddled Kylie's hips. She hovered, blinking in the sudden light, until gravity drew her inexorably downwards with a ghastly tearing sound. The flesh that joined Kylie to Kaylee was no match for the inexorable pull of the earth and slowly split without the support of the pram. Kaylee fell to the ground with a crack, gusts of blood spurting from where she had been excised from Kylie.

As Kaylee fell to earth, she pulled ribbons of purplish innards from her sister, like a macabre conjurer's trick. Kylie stayed on her feet as her intestines unravelled in front of her, shock on her face. The organs continued to spatter at her feet with an awful wet sound, and this was the only thing that broke the silence for a second or two. I don't know what I had expected the innards of two conjoined twins to smell like, but it was truly unique and awful, that stench.

The twins looked at each other then, and a look of true tenderness passed between them. Kylie reached towards her sister, to try to help her at the last, I suppose, but instead, toppled backwards. The movement pulled Kaylee towards her by their shared viscera, the entrails doing the job that Kylie's hands couldn't. Kaylee reached out a stick-thin, withered arm towards the husk of her sister in a final act, and then finally, mercifully, both girls died as they had lived, together.

Someone, I think it was Lee-an, but it could just as well have been me, started to scream.

Author's note

This is a love letter to the stories I grew up reading as a pre-teen, the classics you could find in the wonderful old Pan and Fortuna horror short story anthologies. I hope I have managed to replicate the style and add a little twist of modernity to the mix.

Nuts

The door to the pub blew open, spilling cold air, drizzle, and the shorter of the two into its cosy warm embrace. Stewart (the aforementioned shorty) shuddered, shook and stamped his feet on the mat, glad to be in from the gloomy November night. He automatically looked towards the bar, where he saw both Keith, the landlord, and his lifelong friend, Ted, and smiled. Both were huddled conspiratorially at one end of the mahogany monstrosity. The two were looking towards a third man, sat alone at the table closest to the fireplace, and here Stewart's smile faded. He recognised well the figure sat, peculiarly upright, with a full pint in his hand, and he hurried over to his chums.

"What-ho, chaps," said Stewart as he pulled up a pew. "I was going to ask why you were huddled conspiratorially at the end of the bar, but I see now. Is that…?"

"Neil Q? Yeah," said Keith, eyebrows wriggling dramatically up his forehead. "He just sat down." Without asking, Keith placed a pristine pint of spitfire in front of Stewart and reached for Ted's empty for a refill. Stewart sat down, unable to tear his gaze from the newcomer. Neil, for his part, seemed oblivious to the scrutiny and sat perfectly still, his eyes focused, unblinking, on an object unknown. Ted handed a fiver over and Keith handed his change back, before returning to the huddle.

"How long has he been missing now?" Asked Stewart.

"Little over a week," answered Ted, draining the lion's share of his pint in the first swallow. "This pint is the nectar of the gods."

"Agreed," Stewart said over the rim of his glass. "Did he say anything when he came in?"

"Not a dicky-bird," Keith said, making a great deal of rearranging the glasses behind the bar while surreptitiously keeping a beady one on the interloper. "I asked if he was ok, where he'd been, all that stuff, but he just walked past me and collapsed into the chair with a squeak. I brought him his usual but he didn't even seem interested in that."

Ted and Stewart turned slowly and as sneakily as they could, tried to see what Neil was up to. There he was, stiff as a board, staring unblinking at a spot on the wall just by the lavvy door, near the bookshelf with the well-thumbed paperbacks and occasional board game.

"Did you not call the police? Or the papers? Or even his wife?" Stewart inquired, reasonably.

"No mate, we didn't know when you were coming in and didn't want you to miss out on any excitement his presence caused," replied Ted.

"I will get on the blower with the local plod and let them know we have him," Keith said over his shoulder as he slipped through the faded red curtain and into the mysterious and shadowy area behind the bar.

"I didn't know the pub had a phone," observed Ted.

"You live and learn," shrugged Stew. "I think we should be a bit more clandestine about our observation of Mr Q."

"Good idea," Ted said and turned to face the optics.

After a minute or so of the two trying desperately to see out of their ears, Keith returned, his already keg-shaped physique puffed up noticeably with the pride of civic duty. "Local chaps will be here as soon as they can. They said to try and keep him here if possible. In the meantime, perhaps either of you can fill me in on his story. I know only that he disappeared some days ago, but know nothing of the whys and wherefores."

"Ted here knows more about it than me," chimed Stew.

"Yeah, Neil and I would occasionally pop into town to…" Here Ted's self-preservation instinct kicked in, and he looked up to see the gimlet glare of the landlord. "…go shopping? Shoes and stuff? Never any other pubs, though, of course."

"Of course." Keith's glare lessened. "You never go 'shopping' with them, Stew?"

"Not me. I think old Neil is a bit of a tit," said Stew.

"He's alright once you get to know him. He can be a bit of a loudmouth but his heart is in the right place," Ted opined.

"A bit of a loudmouth? He once told me he killed a mosquito by punching it out of the air."

Stewart shook his head. "Before Ted continues, I fear my beer is no longer here."

"Another for me as well, please Keith," agreed Ted, finishing his last half-inch. The two friends sat in silent reverence as Keith once again performed the sacred ceremony of the pumps.

"I once saw Olivier's Hamlet, you know, and it wasn't a patch on what Keith can do with a pint glass," sighed Ted dreamily.

Once the drinks were delivered and paid for, Ted began, "Anyway, so, what do you know about the whole business?"

"Not a great deal," answered Keith. "Just the bare bones, in fact. Best you start from the beginning."

"Okeydokey." Ted motioned for the other two to draw closer. "So, yeah, Neil. He's alright, but he can be a bit full of himself. Not much to tell really up until maybe two months ago, when he bought the old Wharton place out in the sticks."

"Oh, he bought that place? I thought the general consensus was that place is haunted?" asked Keith.

"True, most people in town do think it's haunted, that's why it had been empty for so long, and also why Neil got it so cheap. I asked him if he was worried about the rumours when he told me he had an offer accepted, and he laughed and said there was no such thing as ghosts, but if there were he would kick them in their spectral spuds and tell them to be on their way."

"Sounds like Neil," tutted Stew.

"Indeed," continued Ted. "Anyway, so, he's doing okay in his building business, he decides to take a punt and buy the Wharton place. He tells me it was going for a song, what with the rumours of the hauntings and all, and once he actually went inside he saw the dilapidation was all cosmetic, but the interior was filled with period fixtures and was structurally sound. He reckons he can fix it up on the cheap, and when it's done it will be the best house in town. So, he makes an offer there and then on his first viewing, and it was accepted. He rushes home to tell the Mrs, who is understandably perplexed, but eventually Neil talks her around and she's on board."

"Now, Kimberley, his Mrs? Her I like," interjected Stew. "I always thought she could do loads better than him. She's like the yin to his yang. Quiet, thoughtful, funny. Yeah, I like her."

"Nothing to do with the way she fills out a pair of Levi's, I suppose?" asked Ted with a raised eyebrow. "Anyway, so, he buys the place. Wanting to free up money for the project he decides its best to move in straight away, live around the workmen kind of thing. So, all is good for the first week or so. Then, late one night, actually, funnily enough while he and I were out shopping—"

"One of those new twenty-four-hour shoe shops they have in the high street, I assume?" asked Keith frostily.

"Enn, yes, quite," said Ted, somewhat red around the ears with guilt. "Anyway, while we were out looking at clogs and espadrilles and whatnot, Kim is at home painting some walls, and she hears something untoward from the loft."

"Was it the ghastly moans of the unquiet dead?" gasped Keith, gripping the bar so hard his chubby pink knuckles turned white.

"Of course, it wasn't, there's no such thing as ghosts," scoffed Ted as he took a swig of spitfire. "No, it was a terrible scratching sound, and it fair put the willies up Kimberley."

"I'd like to put the—" began Stew.

"Yes, thank you, there's no need to bring the tone down. Anyway, so, she's too scared to go check it out, and by the time Neil gets home, he's way too wobbly to climb a ladder to the loft—"

"Do these twenty-four-hour shoe shops also serve alcohol? They do sound wonderful. Please furnish me with the address so I may partake myself, one evening," said a flinty-eyed Keith.

"Ahem, yes, quite, anyway, so, with all the horrible scrabbling and scratching, they have a terrible night. First thing in the morning, as soon as Neil is up to tackling a ladder, up he climbs. And you will never guess what he found up there." Ted smiled at his companions.

"A tragically malformed and forgotten child, chained to the wall and surrounded by the gnawed bones of his missing family?" gulped Keith.

"No, worse." Ted smirked with a ghoulish air.

"A series of hideous marionettes, each more terrifying than the last, whose limbs seemed to move almost imperceptibly despite there being no hint of a draught in the attic?" said Keith, eyes wide.

"No, worse than that."

"A box, shaped suspiciously like a great and ancient sarcophagus, with many bizarre and eldritch sigils carved upon it, and emblazoned with a stamp from Miskatonic University, Arkham?" Keith said in a hushed whisper.

"Worse. Much worse. He found, dun dun dun…" Here Ted paused for dramatic effect and Keith leant forward. "SQUIRRELS!" He boomed.

Keith let out a shriek and leapt backwards. "Oh, you silly arse, you nearly made me pee me kecks!" While Ted and Stew guffawed, Keith made a great show of brushing himself down and regaining his composure. Stew declared this was a good time for a round of fresh refreshing beverages and while Keith performed his art on the pumps, the two friends took the time to use the facilities. On their way, they both nodded a friendly "Alright, mate," at Neil, who didn't register the pair, just sat stiffly staring into the distance. Their beautiful beer was awaiting them on their return and was promptly paid for.

"Anyway, so, as soon as he enters the loft, he disturbs a massive colony of squirrels, who scatter unto the four winds at his entrance, so to speak. Well, he inspected the rafters and beams up there, and discovered no small amount of Sciuridae-related damage."

"Sciuridae?" Stew raised a quizzical brow.

"Sciuridae. Relating to squirrels and their brethren."

"Like I always say, you always learn something down the pub. Please continue." Stew smiled sagely.

"Thank you. Anyway, so. After a grumpy morning with a thick head from the night before, cleaning up squirrel turds and surveying the gnaw marks, old Neil was rightly miffed. His whole weekend was shot, just repairing the damage and trying to seal up all methods of entrance the fluffy-tailed gits had been using to get in and destroy his woodwork. So, as soon as he had repaired the damage, off he popped to homebase to purchase the very latest in squirrel traps. Now, Kim, his Mrs, she was a touch upset at the thought of murdering Tufty, being all kind-hearted and all, but Neil overrode her and pointed out their great and very real danger of them destroying their new house. Reluctantly she was on board."

Ted paused to take a swig from his pint. "The next day, what did Neil find? One dead squirrel. Well, he was made up, but also angry that the devils were still gaining ingress, so he checked again, found no holes, and set some more traps. This went on for quite some time, some days just one adorable corpse, some days two or three, but always something, always a victim. Never finding how they were getting in. So, after a while, he decides he needs to go to the source, take out the nest that he assumed was in the forest outside his house."

"By now, Kim is starting to get a little worried, most of his days are spent plotting the demise of the entire colony, and their bin is so full of fluffy cadavers, she can't fit the potato peelings in. She brings this up, as gently as she can, and Neil agrees that it's not the best way of dealing with the problem. Well, she was expecting him to put them on a bonfire or something, which would've been horrible, but his solution was even worse. She comes back from the supermarket one afternoon to be greeted by a great and terrible stench filling her home. She follows the trail of the pong and traces it to the attic. What does she find up there? Only old Neil, boiling up squirrel carcasses like some kind of low-budget Vincent Price character."

"He's my very favourite," confided Keith to Stew.

"Mine too," said Stew enthusiastically. "There's an argument that Dr Phibes one and two are the greatest achievements in cinematic history. In fact—"

"Ahem." Ted cleared his throat histrionically. "If I may?"

The other two apologised and Ted continued, "So, there he was. He'd taken out a book on taxidermy and was learning the craft up there by himself. Well, Kimberley was not pleased, and even less so once his terrifying creations started to be placed around the house. On one of the last times I visited him at his place, Neil showed me some of his handiwork, and," looking over his shoulder to check Neil wasn't listening, he carried on, "they were awful. Not just his taxidermical skills, which were basic at best, but he'd taken to dressing the poor wee squirrels in costumes and posing them in a manner that paid tribute to his favourite telly shows."

"Dear god," muttered Keith.

"Yup. There was a fuzzy malformed Karl Howman from his brush strokes heyday. One he had fashioned into a reasonable facsimile of Dennis Waterman reprising his masterful performance from 'on the up'. He had made one poor bugger into Paul Daniels and had created a replica 'every second counts' set. On his mantelpiece? A squirrelly Rob Curling behind his turnabout desk. All very wonky and very weird."

"He had killed so many that they had totally stopped trying to get into his house, but he was so into his new hobby that he had taken to going into the woods of an evening and actually hunting the poor sods. Kim and I pointed out that this was unnecessary, he had defended the property, but he was so wrapped up into stuffing squirrels that he refused to listen to reason. He confided to me that he was building up to something, his magnum opus, rendered in the dead flesh of rodents. He wouldn't tell me what it was, only he would need a very great deal of dead squirrels to manage it."

"Well, I made a sharp exit, and didn't really hear from old Neil for a few weeks until I ran into him at the all-night shoe shop I mentioned previously." Ted caught a glimpse of Keith's scowl and continued, "There was Neil, looking as happy as hell and drunk as a badger. He bought me a pint and ushered me over to a table, where he explained the reason for his cheerful inebriation. Turns out he'd not seen a squirrel in days, thought he'd killed them all. This had sent him into despair as he was only halfway through his furtive masterwork, now doomed to incompletion due to lack of dead 'uns."

"Anyway, he told me he'd been in a right old funk, thinking he would never finish. Said he'd gone further into the woods and nothing. Said he'd looked into buying dead squirrels on the internet. Nothing. Said he'd even tried to use rats and other rodents, but they just didn't have the charm of old nutkins. Said he was just about to give up and throw out all of his work in despair, when fate showed her hand. A man had approached him on the internet, on one of the taxidermy message boards he frequented. Said for the princely sum of a hundred quid he would sell him the ultimate squirrel lure, all he had to do was collect it. Well, Neil had set off the very next day, all the way to Sherwood Forest on the train. He'd had to change at Ashford, of course."

"Of course," agreed Stew and Keith.

"But the bloke had met him in a pub and sold him the lure. Now, when he showed it to me, it looked like a child's recorder crudely painted with pictures of acorns and such, but Neil said he'd made the chap show him how it worked before he would fork over the cash. Said the fellow took him to the car park behind the pub and blew a quick blast. Neil's face lit up when he told me what happened next, he said after a few moments these three squirrels trotted out of the skip behind the pub, went over to the bloke, and just sort of stood there, swaying slightly, like they were hypnotised, or something."

"Neil was amazed, and was about to knock the three on the head when the bloke blew another blast and the three turned tail and scampered away as fast as their delightfully cute little toes could take them. Neil asked the bloke, and he said he carved the lures himself. He had studied squirrels his entire life, and had made a rudimentary study of their language, such as it was. And this child's recorder essentially made the most enticing sound a squirrel could ever hear. Well, I thought that sounded like a fool being parted from his hundred nicker by a charlatan with three trained squirrels, but I kept my counsel, what with Neil being all effusive and drunk and eager to buy me beer, and all."

"Talking of which…" Stewart examined his empty glass forlornly, "time for another and a swift trot to the bog."

Pints were pulled, urine was extracted, Neil ignored them again, and presently everyone was back in their seats for the thrilling denouement.

"So, anyway," Ted continued, "he disappeared not too long after that, about a week ago. I went over a day or so later, to see if I could help, and the rest of the story comes from Kim. She says he had been as happy as she'd ever seen him, and the lure had worked spectacularly well for about three days. He'd gone to stand in the back garden by the trees, blown on the recorder thingy like the fellow had shown him, and a horde of squirrels would scamper down from the trees."

"Neil would wring their cute little necks and bung them in a bag. No sooner had he gathered up a sackful then he would be back, blowing on his lure and murdering rodents. Sort of like a homicidally inclined inverse pied piper, I suppose. Anyway, she said late on the second evening, the squirrels started to get less and less. He had actually committed fuzzy genocide on such a scale, he had emptied the forest. There were no more victims within range of his tooting. Kimberley said he was like a man possessed, and spent the whole night pacing the house muttering about how he didn't have enough, how his life's work was ruined. Well, she went to bed leaving him to his mania. She said she was woken up in the early hours of the third day, with Neil's side of the bed empty."

"At first, she thought she was dreaming, but nope, she sat upright and there it was, a woman's voice. She said it sounded very odd, quite scratchy and squeaky. Well, she couldn't make out the words at first, but she crept closer to the window and she could clearly hear what the woman was saying. It was coming from the forest at the back of the house, and she said she could hear the voice talking to Neil, saying things like, 'Come to me, Neil, I will satisfy your every sordid whim' and 'I have a case of that expensive lager you like' and 'Let's go for a kebab.'"

"Now, old Neil had been known to have trouble keeping his little chap in his trousers before, so Kimberley assumed it was one of his fancy bits come to entice him away. She slipped on her dressing gown and thundered down the stairs, ready to give the trollop and her wayward husband what for. As she got to the bottom of the stairs, she heard the back door bang shut. *That bastard! He'd gone off with his bit on the side*, she thought. So, ever the traditionalist, she grabbed her rolling pin and charged out to confront the pair. What did she see when she got outside? Nothing. Not a trace. She went into the woods a way, but it was dark and cold, so she only got a few steps, but no sign of the pair. She went back inside, made herself a cup of coffee, and awaited Neil's return, with full intention of committing intense violence upon his hapless person."

"Well, he never showed, not that day, nor the next. She went into the woods to look but she said there was no sign at all, just an eerie silence. After a while, she reported him missing to the police, and they checked, and found no sign of him, and his bank account and such were untouched. He had pretty much vanished into thin air. Until tonight, of course." Ted leant back on his stool and took a well-earned drink.

Stewart and Keith looked at each other, then at Neil, still bolt upright, still staring into space.

"Where do you think he's been?" asked Keith in an excited tone.

"I think he ran off with some young dolly bird, forgetting his age, and she's rogered him into a semi-comatose state," opined Stew.

At that very moment, the ornamental bell above the pub door jangled its cheery refrain and the imposing figure of P.C. Greenlee, the local copper, strode in. He nodded to the trio at the bar in a curt, business-like fashion, and strode directly to the table Neil was sat at.

"Looks like we may get some answers after all," said Ted, as the three settled back for a spot of free theatre.

"Now then, sir. May I ask where you have been these last few days?" Boomed Greenlee.

Neil just sat and stared, didn't flinch or move.

"Sir. I would rather you helped me out by answering a few informal questions here, then I can get you home to your wife, who I imagine has some questions of her own. Now, where have you been? Do you require medical attention?" Nothing.

"Sir. If you choose not to help me here then I will have to ask you to accompany me to the station."

The three at the bar were all agog.

"Sir." This the big burly copper said in a very intimidating tone. He stepped forward and placed his hand on Neil's bicep. With a ghastly tearing sound, Neil's arm came away in his hand. Greenlee looked, dumbfounded, as a small form covered in blood and ichor wriggled from the amputated arm, then skittered across the pub, leaving bloody footprints as it went. It reached the window and all four men watched, struck motionless with horror, as it threw itself against the glass, once, twice, leaving a sticky morass of blood and ooze on the pane. As the gore flew from its fur, it became apparent to them all what this was. A squirrel.

On the third attempt, the glass broke and the blood-covered rodent burst through into the cold wet November night. All four slowly, as one, turned to look at the husk of Neil. Slowly, inexorably, impossibly tiny stitches started to give way. Neil's skin started to flap and fall like a banana peel, revealing dozens and dozens of blood-drenched squirrels, which started to flow like some foul plague from one of Terry Nutkins' nightmares towards the broken window. After a matter of seconds, they were gone, the once pristine pub now covered in a myriad of tiny, bloody footprints.

Ashen-faced, Ted turned to the other two. "I didn't know squirrels could sew," he said in a leaden tone.

"Like I say, you always learn something new in the pub," said Stewart, nimbly hopping off his stool. He started to pull his jacket on.

"Are you going somewhere, Stew?" Asked Keith, unable to tear his eyes, rounded as they were with terror, from the skin suit that pooled grotesquely on the pub floor.

"Well, I thought I'd go and see Kimberley, check she's okay, how she's adapting to her new status as a widow and all."

Officer Greenlee took a long look at the peeled arm in his hand, the opera glove from hell, and vomited copiously on the floor.

Author's note

This is a love letter to one of the greatest short horror stories ever, Nigel Kneale's *The Pond*. Though more famous as the creator of *Quatermass*, his short fiction is always impressive and imaginative. I first discovered *The Pond* in Ramsay Campbell's fantastic anthology, *The Gruesome Book*, one of my favourites growing up. I still have my original paperback from 1983. If you enjoyed *Nuts*, you will love *The Pond*.

Mr Greendale's Oak Tree

"He's always here, hanging around when the kids are playing," said Shirley to her sister, her lip curled with thinly veiled contempt.

"Who? Oh, that old bloke? Greendale? Yes, I suppose he is. But isn't that his house over there? I mean, the gate in his back fence is right there, it opens up to here directly. I would be here all the time too if it was that convenient for me," Deborah replied, briefly glancing over her copy of Celeb magazine.

"Well, that's different." Shirley waved vaguely towards a scrum of children playing on a patch of grass by the old oak tree. "I think it's weird. He just sits there, watching our kids and fiddling around with all that horrible rubbish he brings with him. It's not right. And he's always telling the kids off if they try and climb the tree."

Deborah sighed and put down her magazine. She loved her sister, but it was a difficult job sometimes.

"He has every right to be here. This is the only public land in the village, and if he wants to spend his days sat there then let him. Let's count our blessings, he seems nice enough, he could be sat in the house writing letters of complaint to the parish council every five minutes complaining about our noisy kids just outside his back fence. The tree is old, and the kids shouldn't climb it. If a kid fell out, the council would cut it down, and that would be a shame. And he's lived here longer than us. Longer than everyone else in the village, actually."

"I don't see why he doesn't spend his time with his own kids, instead of bothering ours," grumbled Shirley.

"Because his kid went missing forty-odd years ago!" said Deborah with a slight gasp at her sister's callousness. "You know that!"

"Oh. Yeah," Shirley conceded the point begrudgingly. "Well, I just think it's fishy, is all." And, rising to her feet from the bench and picking up her carrier bag that contained the spoils of today's trip to the local shop, shouted, "Matt? Lucy? Time to go. See you tomorrow, Debs, I will call you tonight after supper for a chat to sort out what we are doing with the kids on their break next week." And with that, she strolled away.

Two days later was a Saturday, and Shirley had arranged for both families to meet at the park for a picnic. Shirley, her husband Dave, and the two kids were first there, and Deborah was unsurprised to see they had the park to themselves. It was a very small village, and most people headed out to the bigger towns on the weekends, searching for something to do, or buy. It had taken a great deal of persuasion to get her husband, Mike, to agree to the picnic, as he had no time for her sister or brother-in-law. Begrudgingly, he had agreed, mainly out of love for her.

Their two daughters, Claire and Laura, didn't much care for their cousins either and would have been happier at home with their phones, and Deborah had started to feel, as she chivvied them along, that maybe they were the ones in the right. But family is family, and here they were. They walked past Mr Greendale's back fence, which occupied the whole of the south end of the park, to approach the bench.

"Only two hours tops, right, love?" murmured Mike in her ear. "I want to catch the game on the telly this afternoon."

"Yes, and I bought you some extra beer to go with the match for going through with this," she smiled in return. Mike's beam of happiness made her giggle, and they were both laughing as they approached her sister and family. Shirley sat on the bench, watching Dave play football with Matt and smoking a cigarette. Deborah couldn't fail to notice that while she had turned up in her jeans and a sweatshirt, Shirley had pulled out an expensive looking summer frock and pair of heels totally unsuited to a lunchtime in the park.

Shirley waved at them as they approached and Deborah smiled and waved back. Deborah's daughters ran off to help their cousin Lucy with the preposterously long daisy chain she was constructing, and she and Mike greeted Shirley and waved at the rest of her family, before she sat on the bench next to her sister, Mike placing the picnic hamper at his feet. Dave kicked the ball to Matt and jogged over, sweat glistening on his face.

"Alright Debs? Looking good. Mikey! How they hanging?" With that, Dave feinted a punch to Mike's testicles. Mike crumpled defensively, causing howls of laughter from Dave and a snort of amusement from Shirley. Dave hugged Mike in a sweaty embrace, and over his shoulder Mike glared at Deborah. Dave caught sight of the hamper and instantly broke the hug and started rummaging around inside it, before coming up with a can of lager. He popped the tab and drained half in a swallow.

"Please, help yourself," muttered Mike in a voice so low only Deborah could hear.

"Oh here he comes, knew he couldn't keep away," Shirley crowed, as she pointed towards Mr Greendale's back gate. Sure enough, the gate opened and the familiar angular figure of Greendale shuffled out. He was old, but tall, and his hair, though snow white, was thick and full, which was more than could be said for Dave's. His green tweed suit was dated, but immaculate, and he walked stiffly, almost jerkily, like a tall thin bird. He raised a hand in greeting to the four of them, before slowly and deliberately settling in his usual bench close to the oak tree, a good forty or so yards away.

They all watched as he pulled a handful of items out of his inner pocket, which he spent some time arranging on the bench next to him. Seemingly pleased with their arrangement, Greendale turned his attention to the children playing in the lee of the great oak. The three girls sat by its roots, picking daisies, while the only boy child, Matt, a clone of his father with his egg-shaped body and fat face, his lips a cruel thin slash always turned in a sneer it seemed, dribbled his football inexpertly between them.

"What's that, Shirl? Old Greendale? He been giving you and the kids trouble?" Dave asked, glaring towards the old man.

"Not at all," answered Deborah, cutting off her sister before she had a chance to reply. "Shirley just noticed that he's often here when the kids play."

"Not often, always. I just don't think it's right, is all. Old man like that, on his tod, always hanging around when the little ones are there. Who knows what's on his mind." Shirley sniffed, fumbling in her handbag for a cigarette to replace the one she had just ground out with her heel.

"It's a public park, Shirley," noted Mike, while privately marvelling at Shirley's use of the phrase little ones to describe her massive offspring. "Maybe seeing the kids play makes him happier, after his kid. You know. What harm is he doing?" But Dave's eyes had narrowed.

"You think he's a nonce, Shirl?" He bristled.

"I'm not saying that. I am just saying, seems to me a bit strange that as soon as he sees the kids coming to play by the tree, he rushes out of his horrid little house and gets settled on his bench, with all his weird stuff out of his pocket. We don't know what is going through his mind, do we?" She glanced around conspiratorially and added in a stage whisper, "It's not like they ever found out what happened to his kid."

Deborah gasped in surprise at the lack of empathy from her sister, and was about to pull her up on it, but wisely kept her counsel.

"Sounds like a paedo to me. You're right, Shirl, I will keep an eye on him," Dave said, before rummaging through the hamper and coming up with a sandwich wrapped in tin foil. "What's in this?"

"They are all ham and mustard," Deb replied, pleased Dave had been distracted.

"Bloody hell, you know I don't like ham, it disagrees with my guts, don't it, Shirl?" Dave said, disappointed.

"Maybe eat something you brought yourself, then," grumbled Mike, again just low enough to be out of earshot.

"Oh well, you lot will have to just deal with my farts. I'm starving," Dave said, unwrapping the foil and stuffing a mouthful in.

The four settled into the usual banal pleasantries, dominated by Shirley and her one-upmanship and Dave's inelegant braggadocio. Mike had switched off from the conversation almost immediately, and Deborah followed not long after, her ears tuning out the drone of her sister making some cruel comment or another about one of the other mums in the village. A rhythmic thudding dragged her back to attention, and she noted that Matt had taken to kicking his football against Mr Greendale's fence, a look of sullen boredom on his face.

"Hey, Shirl, should Matty be doing that?" Deborah asked.

Shirley scowled at her sister, annoyed that she had been interrupted mid-monologue, and glanced over to her son.

"He's fine, look, the old weirdo isn't worried so why should you be? Anyway, where was I?" She said, before returning to her diatribe. Deborah looked, and Shirl was right. Mr Greendale was watching the boy, he was close enough to call out, but he seemed not to care. *Oh well*, thought Deborah, *if he wants the boy to stop, he will surely let us know*.

"Matt? Oi, Matty!" shouted Dave to his son. Matt stopped what he was doing and looked to his father. "Give it some welly, lad! You're kicking like a poofter!" Dave smiled at Mike like he had imparted a quip worthy of Wilde. Matt raised two thumbs up, placed his ball on the ground, and after a brief inelegant run up, kicked the ball with all his might into Mr Greendale's fence. The ball cannoned off, shot back over his head, and lodged in the lowest bough of the oak tree.

"Look at that! Kid's a natural. Got a shot like super Harry!" Dave chuckled, nudging Mike in the ribs as he did so. Mike glanced up and saw Matt give a 'what are you going to do?' shrug and trudge over to the tree.

"Looks like Mr Greendale is going to give him a hand getting his ball back," Mike observed.

"What?" grunted Dave. He followed Mike's pointed finger and saw Greendale rise out of his seat and move over to Matt, his hands out, warding him off. "He's saying something, too far away to hear."

"Oh, Dave, I don't like it, I don't like him talking to our Matty," twittered Shirley. "Go over and see what he wants."

"Oh, it's okay, he's not going to abduct the boy, we can keep an eye on them from here," griped Dave, not wanting to get off his arse. All four adults watched as Matt approached the tree, but Mr Greendale, moving much faster than before, and indeed much faster than they would have given him credit for, intercepted him and stood between him and the ball. Matt made to go around him, but he put his tall body between him and the ball again.

"Dave!" Shirley screamed. "Get over there right now! He's talking to your son. Go!"

Dave struggled to his feet, and with a similar shrug to Mike as Matt had just given him, started to trudge over.

"Oi!" he shouted. "Greendale. What you want with my kid?"

At the sound of his name, Mr Greendale turned towards Dave. Matt saw his chance and made to dart past Greendale and grab his ball. Greendale spun around and, quick as a snake, he pushed Matt. The boy fell on his fat backside, a look of almost comical shock on his face, his mouth a perfectly round O.

"Oi!" bellowed Dave, and he charged towards the old man.

"Oh my god, he hit Matty!" screamed Shirley to her sister, shrill as a kettle. "You saw him! Come on!" She leapt from the bench and chased after Dave, only to stop after a few paces when her heels sank into the earth.

Totally unsuited to a lunchtime in the park, thought Deborah absentmindedly as she overtook her sister and hared towards Matt, followed closely by her husband.

"You fucking old nonce, you keep your hands off my boy," barked Dave. Although a good six inches shorter than the older man, he had his arms spread open, while bounced on the tips of his toes, chest puffed out like a fat bantam chicken. Mr Greendale had his hands in front of him in a calming gesture.

"Please, look, the free is dangerous. I will get the ball for the boy. I didn't want him to get hurt." Mike pulled up behind Dave and put a hand on his shoulder.

"Dave, calm down," said Mike gently. "It's not worth it."

Dave shrugged off Mike's hand and put his finger in Mr Greendale's face. "You do not touch my kids. Ever."

"Please, look, it's not safe. The tree is old. Let me get the ball." Greendale turned and reached out to get the ball.

Dave grabbed him by the shoulder and spun him around, the old man tottered but didn't fall.

"Don't you turn your fucking back on me, you piece of shit paedo."

"Dave, stop," panted Deborah, just arriving. "He just wants to get the ball for him, that's all."

Dave paused a beat, his anger leaving him. "Well, go on then," he spat in Greendale's face.

Greendale looked puzzled. "Go on then what?"

"Get. The. Fucking. Ball. From. The. Tree." Each word punctuated by a jab of the finger into the old man's chest. Mr Greendale coiled away from the contact.

"Oh right, of course." He turned, and effortlessly pulled the ball from the branch and handed it to Dave.

"Now apologise," Shirley snarled, pulling up behind her husband, her shoes abandoned yards away. "Apologise for touching my boy."

Mr Greendale looked from face to face. He saw vicious anger in Shirley and Dave. Deborah and Mike both looked encouragingly, smiling, willing him to say sorry and defuse the situation. The three girls sat in identical open-mouthed shock, the daisy chain forgotten across their laps. Matt had a look of vindictive smugness plastered across his face.

"I am sorry. I didn't mean to hurt the boy. Is he alright?"

Directly on cue, Matt started to cry. Big, whooping sobs.

Shirley shot Mr Greendale a look of pure hatred and hustled over to comfort her offspring.

"Are you happy now? Mister bigshot, making a little kid cry. You should be fucking ashamed of yourself. Or maybe that's what gets you off? Eh? That what floats your boat, crying kids? Disgusting old pervert," Dave growled, puffing himself up again.

"Dave, look, no harm done eh?" said Mike as he deftly inserted himself between the two. "Come on, mate, calm down, eh? Let's go get another can of lager."

This calmed Dave and he started to allow Mike to shepherd him away. Shirley, however, was in no mood to be calmed.

"No harm done? No harm done, Mike?" She glowered, getting to her feet. There was such menace, cold and sharp in her voice, that all turned to her. Even Matt forgot to keep up his crocodile tears.

"My son, your nephew, is crying because this man hit him, and you call that nothing?"

Deborah recognised that tone in her sister's voice and knew she must step in now, or things would go even further downhill.

"Shirl, come on now, look—"

"You? You I expect weakness from," Shirley snarled at her sister, "but Mike, well, I thought he was more of a man. Looks like I was wrong." Shirley stepped towards the old man now, her small bony fists bunched at her side. "But that doesn't matter now. What matters is what this old ponce is doing in the park, every day, watching my kids. And why he thinks he's entitled to touch my children."

"I assure you I mean no-one any harm," said Mr Greendale as he backed away from Shirley. She was advancing on him now so quickly that she was forcing him back, back towards his bench.

"I assure you I mean blah blah blah," mimicked Shirl in a ghastly sing-song voice. "Well, that means fuck all when you've already punched my kid, does it?"

Mr Greendale's long bony legs bumped against the bench. He turned around momentarily at the contact. Shirley noticed his attention drop and pushed him firmly with both hands on his chest. He fell, seated, on the bench with a gasp and a wince of pain. She looked around at the others, a gleam of triumph on her thin, nasty face.

"So now we're even, by my reckoning, Mr fucking Greendale, eh? You hit my kid, now I've hit you." She leant closer to him, so close that their noses nearly touched. For one bizarre moment, Deborah thought her sister was going to kiss the old man. "But let me tell you, if I see you here watching my kids, for whatever fucking reason, I will personally cut your bollocks off with my nail scissors, do you understand me?" Shirley hissed from between her teeth. "And what the fuck is this crap?" She dropped her hand from his face and pointed towards the collection of trinkets and junk Mr Greendale had arranged on the bench next to him, five minutes and a lifetime ago.

Deborah was shocked to see the change that came over Mr Greendale. When Dave had confronted him, he looked worried. When Shirley had marched him across to the bench, he looked scared. But now, now he looked terrified. Deborah looked at where Shirley pointed, and for the first time registered what the old man had placed on the bench. There were about a dozen pieces in total, and all similar. What looked like small pieces of bone, possibly chicken, with a sprig of plant tied to it with a small thin strip of red ribbon. The plant looked familiar, with its pale green stem and leaves, and white berries, but Deborah couldn't place where she'd seen it before.

"What is this disgusting shit?" Spat Shirley. She reached forward to pick up a bone. Before anyone had time to react the old man, moving as quick as a viper, swatted Shirley's hand away.

"Bastard!" shouted Dave, and lunged towards the old man. Mike tried to grab at him but it was too late. Dave threw a clumsy overhand punch that landed on the old man's nose with an audible crunch, like a bag of crisps that had been stepped on. Blood splattered immediately from his face, and Mr Greendale recoiled into the bench, both nostrils now gushing the sticky red liquid over his lips.

Deborah watched in horror as fat, glossy red drips started to fall from his chin onto his once pristine suit.

"What the fuck, Dave?" shouted Mike, as he started to drag the smaller man back.

"You saw. The cunt hit Shirl," Dave bellowed.

"He pushed her hand away. Jesus," Deborah said, stepping in between Dave and the bench. Dimly, she registered the sound of crying behind her. It sounded like Laura.

"Well, I should've guessed you'd side with this old perv over your own blood," snapped Shirley. "You've always thought you're better than me and Dave, you and your snooty dickless husband. Well, you're not. And as for you." She pointed a finger over her sister's shoulder at the old man, who was shaking his head groggily, drops of blood flying in all directions. "As for you, you're lucky I don't press charges. If you know what's good for you, you'll never let me catch you here again." And with that, she picked up the bones in both hands and threw them as far as she could. Instantly they disappeared into the long grass. "Come on, Dave, kids. We are leaving." She spun on her heel and started marching off.

"Wait," croaked the old man. Shirley stopped in her tracks. "Wait." Mr Greendale shook his head again and unsteadily climbed to his feet. He gave a great sniff and a cough, and hocked a huge glob of bloody mucus on the ground, barely missing his own shoes. Blood covered most of his face from top lip downwards, and seeped into the fabric of his clothes, but his eyes flashed with rage, and Shirley took an involuntary step back from the ferocity he radiated. He raised a shaky finger and pointed at her.

"You will never see me here again, you have my word. For forty-three years, since my beloved daughter disappeared, I have sat and guarded the children of this village from sharing her fate. My wife passed in that time, and still I sat here. Through rain and snow, I sat here. Because what took my daughter lives in this tree." He coughed and spat more blood. "But I am done. This is the final straw. I am an old man who deserves some joy in the last few years of his life. So I am out." He turned to Deborah, and too quietly for the others to hear, whispered, "Never let your children play in the tree." With that, gasping in pain, the old man awkwardly made his way to his back fence and slammed the gate closed.

Later that evening, after the girls had gone to bed, Mike and Deborah had a chance to talk.

"Well," said Mike over his beer, "what happens now?"

"I reckon we just carry on," said Deborah. "I won't contact them, and I'm sure they won't contact us. To be honest, we all knew a falling out was coming, I just didn't expect it like that. And if you're honest, you must be quite glad."

Mike smiled. "Yeah, I won't be weeping about never hearing Dave's awesome collection of racist jokes ever again. Will you be okay though, love?"

"Yeah, I will be fine. The only thing we had in common was biology. I loved her, but I think it was mainly out of duty.

The kids will be fine, they didn't like their cousins much anyway, I think they are relieved like you, to be honest. I'm just so shocked and surprised at the amount of resentment they had towards us."

"Did you hear what he said? Greendale? What do you think he meant about something living in the tree?" asked Mike. "Do you think he was in shock and just babbling? Should we go and check he's okay in the morning? Nasty knock like that could've been a concussion."

"I have no idea. He whispered something to me as well, just as he left, about not allowing the kids to play on the tree," Deborah said. "I wonder what that's about?"

"I dunno, but let's stay clear of the park, eh? Less chance of running into your sister if we give it a skip for a while."

"It's going to be tough with the kids off next week, but I'm sure we can think of something else to do," Deborah agreed, and soon they sank into a comfortable silence in front of the television.

Three days later, Matt disappeared.

Shirley had taken the kids to the park that morning and sat with great deliberation on the bench so often occupied by Mr Greendale. They were the only ones there again, and though she kept an eye on the back gate, Mr Greendale never showed his face. She had half hoped that her sister would show, spoiling as she was for round two, but deep down she knew Deb was way too cowardly to show up here. Yeah, they showed them alright, and now her kids had the park to themselves. A wail of sadness interrupted her thoughts and she looked up to see Matt indulging in one of his favourite hobbies—tormenting his younger sister.

"Matt, leave Lucy alone. Go play by the tree." After a second, she added, "Actually, you can play in the tree now, that old busybody isn't here to stop you."

Matt gave a big smile and lumbered the few paces to the low branch. He jumped and caught hold of the bough, but didn't have the strength in his arms to hoist his fat body up. After a few seconds of struggling, he kicked his feet against the trunk, and using the knots and bark for purchase, finally climbed up into the foliage. His mother watched him for a few seconds, before losing interest and glancing at her magazine. When she looked up, he was no longer on the branch. She assumed he had climbed higher still and thought nothing of it. A few more minutes passed, and still no sign. She frowned in puzzlement.

"Luce? Can you see your brother?"

Lucy looked around, then peered into the tree. She shook her head and, with a shrug, went back to her game.

A primal part of Shirley told her something wasn't right. She got up swiftly, her magazine fluttering to her feet, and walked to the base of the tree. She looked directly up. Nothing. "Matt? Matty?" She shouted.

Nothing. "Matt? Come down now." Nothing.

Lucy cocked her head at the increasing note of panic in her mother's voice and stood up, her game forgotten. She stood next to her mother and looked up into the tree. "Matt?" she called out. Nothing.

The police came quickly and examined the tree, but there were no signs, no hint Matt had ever been there. Of course, Shirley pointed a finger at Mr Greendale, and he was taken in for questioning, but he had been away all day, at his lawyer's office, arranging the start of the sale of his house. Days turned into weeks, and Mr Greendale moved away, away from the village that his family had always lived in.

Dave took the disappearance hard. For all his faults, he loved his son, and when he wasn't searching the countryside, he took to drinking more and more and more. Eventually, Shirley left with Lucy to start anew, but Dave never stopped looking.

Long after the police stopped, long after everyone forgot about Matt, you could find what was left of Dave, sitting in the last place his son was seen alive, the park, on the bench where Mr Greendale had once sat, looking at the tree. He thought he had found all of the bones Shirley had thrown that day, but he couldn't be sure. He arranged them on the bench all the same, futilely attempting to recreate the order Greendale had placed them in from that one brief glimpse, a lifetime ago.

If a child went to climb up into the branches of Mr Greendale's oak tree, Dave would immediately rush across and stop them.

Invasive Species

"Brother, do you sleep?" Basav said, his whisper seeming loud in the quiet of the forest morning.

"I wake, my brother," Jeetu responded, rising stiffly from the nest of leaves he had made himself the night before. The moisture of the forest air was heavy, and Jeetu's black hessian pyjamas clung to his body with sweat and dew. Jeetu spent some seconds brushing the leaf mulch from his skin and clothes before walking the few steps across the clearing to where Basav squatted. Basav passed Jeetu a water bottle, which Jeetu drank from greedily, and a handful of berries and mushrooms which he had gathered while Jeetu slept.

"Delicious breakfast, thank you, Basav."

"Kali be praised," Basav muttered, his eyes flickering towards the iron grey sky, just visible through the tree canopy.

"Kali be praised," Jeetu responded automatically. The men had lit no fire, but both seemed unaffected by the cold, damp autumnal air.

"This forest is as a barren desert compared to our lush jungle," Basav said, for the thousandth time it seemed to Jeetu. "The fruits and berries are as ashes in my mouth, compared to the beautiful ripe fruits of home." Basav held a cherry up to a shaft of sunlight. "Look at this pitiful thing, this cherry. It is smaller than a mango stone and tastes just as bad."

"I quite like them." Jeetu smiled. "And we should be grateful for anything that Kali provides us."

"Quite so," Basav agreed, "but I do wish Kali would see to provide us with something that at least didn't taste of jackal shit."

Jeetu laughed. "Now, when did you ever taste jackal shit, Brother Basav?"

"You'd be surprised," Basav said in mock seriousness before a large smile crossed his broad face.

Jeetu looked at Basav and smiled. He was glad he was with him. Jeetu was a big man by anyone's standards, but Basav was huge, a good three inches taller and double the size around the chest it seemed. Underneath the pyjamas, Jeetu knew that like himself, Basav had not an ounce of fat and his body was hard muscle, like it had been sculpted from mahogany. Jeetu had been glad he had been paired with Basav, they had been good friends growing up together in the temple. He would never admit it, but sometimes the strangeness of this forest, this land caused him agitation, and the massive frame of Basav was a reassurance.

"At the very least, Brother, this forest doesn't make us contend with any beasts that could hurt us." Jeetu smiled, then after a second, added, "Except for the pigs, of course."

"Hah!" Basav grinned, "The pigs here can't hurt you, Brother Jeetu. Kali watches over you."

"Well, I hope she turns her eyes from this." Jeetu stood up from his squat, stretched his legs and walked behind the nearest tree. A second or two later, Basav heard the unmistakable sound of urination.

"The monsoon is fierce back home in India, Brother Jeetu. I hear it all the way from here." Basav smiled. He liked Jeetu. The smaller man was good company, and this far from the temple, that was worth its weight in gold. Jeetu reappeared from behind the tree, tying the rumal, the bright yellow ceremonial sash, tightly around the waist of his clothes. The sash was the only thing on the men that had any colour, and its brightness attracted the eye. Basav had worried about the sash, worried it would alert the pigs as they stalked them, but after twenty-four nights here, they had not been spotted once. Kali demanded the sash, and so she blinded the pigs to it, he supposed.

Basav started to gather their possessions up, as meagre as they were, and stored them in the two sacks that they carried with them. The sacks were made from the same hessian as their clothes and were showing some signs of wear after this length of time. Basav was especially worried about his forming a hole and becoming useless, as they still had four days to go on this expedition before making their way back to the collection point. His sack carried the sacred pickaxe, the only sharp metal they had on them, and was wearing accordingly.

If it was the will of Kali that he was to spend the rest of his time in this forest trying to carry everything in one sack, so be it, he thought, however, he failed to see how his annoyance would honour her. He passed the lighter of the two sacks to Jeetu, who slung it nonchalantly across his shoulders.

"Where shall we hunt today, Brother Basav?" Jeetu enquired. They had both spent the same amount of time studying with the guru, they had both achieved the level of bhuttote, yet Jeetu always deferred to Basav, despite arguably being the better tracker of the two, and definitely the more intelligent.

"We have four nights left until they come for us, Brother. Let us start heading back west."

Shrugging unconcernedly, Jeetu started heading west.

Ursula woke up to find everyone she had ever loved was dead. She was in front of the ruins of her family's cottage with no idea how she had come to be there. A big, friendly face covered in a gingery scrub of beard beamed down at her.

"Ho, there, little one. I am surprised but glad to see you are still with us," boomed the healthy voice of the soldier. He helped her to sit up before shouting to persons unseen that he had a survivor. She looked around her in shock, her hands covered in dirt and blood, her face tight and hot. Her village had been flattened, as if by the foot of an ancient god. No building stood, most were on fire.

Four other men arrived quickly, all in the same Wehrmacht uniform of the friendly man who had found her, who identified himself as Horst as he handed her his canteen. Three of the soldiers, two boys and a ratty looking older man, stood silently as the fourth, obviously the man in charge, crouched next to her and looked her over with an air of professional disinterest. Ursula was deaf to his gentle questions as he probed her wounds, but she winced when he touched her face, and understood that she had been burnt.

She had sat silently initially, refusing or unable to answer the questions set to her by the young soldier who identified himself as Unterfeldwebel Mayer, the man she understood to be in charge. He was an unlikely candidate for command, she had thought, he looked young, and nervous, his meticulously clean appearance an obvious reaction to the filth and horror they had found themselves in. After a while, the soldiers had lost interest in her silence and set about scavenging the remains of her village, loading anything of value onto the cart. None spoke to her after the initial questions from Mayer, and she found herself sat by the well in the centre of the village as they went about her business. Horst approached her again, his happy round face almost impossible to be afraid of. He had silently placed some bread and cheese in front of her and was turning to leave, when she found her voice.

"It was a bomb, I think," she had uttered hoarsely.

Horst had said nothing, just smiled at the pretty teenage girl with the blonde hair and the burns on her face and left to find Mayer. When he arrived, the floodgates of her memory had opened and she told him everything. It had happened in the middle of the night, she said in a hoarse, confused whisper, one minute she was asleep in bed, the next the entire village was destroyed. She remembered walking out of the rubble and passing out, nothing more. The soldier had no idea of the date, so neither of them could pinpoint how long she had been out, but Mayer surmised that it had been at least a day, probably more. She had been lucky, in a way, he explained, the damp weather had probably restricted most of the fires and had kept her safe.

Mayer explained the most likely explanation was a bomber flying back to Britain, having finished a night raid, had decided to jettison its payload over the forest to lighten their load on the homeward leg. Probably someone had lit a fire, and the pilot had seen it, and that was the end of everyone that Ursula had ever cared about. A regular occurrence, he shrugged. He fetched a first aid kit from one of the others and set about patching her wounds. He told her it was all superficial, that the burns to her face would heal, in time. She had half a dozen cuts that required cleaning as well, all of which she dealt with with a quiet fortitude that impressed Mayer.

As he cleaned her cuts and found her dry clothes, he talked. He explained that the Allies were fast approaching Berlin, and all units had been recalled to protect the capital. His unit, or what was left of it, were doing exactly that. He seemed optimistic that they would repel the invaders and still win the war, but his eyes seemed glassy, and it seemed more jingoistic optimism than reality. He had asked what Ursula's plans were, now that she was homeless here in the forest, and she admitted she had none. He inquired after any skills she may have and upon learning she had studied English had insisted she came with them to Berlin.

"You could help us negotiate a surrender if we encounter the British." He smiled.

She sat, emotionless as she watched her friends' possessions get loaded onto the cart, uncaring and unmindful of the looting. Horst had come to get her when they had worked their way to her family home, and had watched as she picked through the rubble. She had rescued some photos, some clothes, nothing of value to anyone else. After five minutes, she had finished and Horst had helped her back to the cart, mercifully out of sight of the others scavenging the corpse of her home. A few hours later and they were done, and Ursula was in the back of the cart, where she almost instantly fell asleep.

Ursula opened one eye, very slightly, not wishing any of the soldiers to see she was conscious. She was lying in the crude wooden cart, the rough wood and splinters slapping against her every time it encountered a rut or pothole on the forest track. Raising her head a little further, she could make out the possessions and valuables that surrounded her, such as they were. She rolled over and lay on her back, the early afternoon sky above her iron grey through the canopy of pine and elm. A light drizzle was falling, and it felt good on the hot dry skin of her face.

Tilting her head towards the front of the cart, she recognised the horse as being that which belonged to Karl, the miller, by its patch of white on the back of its neck. Karl had been the father of Piotr, a boy she liked but was too shy to tell, and she knew she would never get a chance to tell him now. She realised she was thirsty, thirstier than she had ever been, it felt, and turned her head from side to side slowly, as not to attract attention, looking for water. Nothing but clothes, some paintings, small pieces of furniture. She recognised the small lamp that her aunt had kept in her front room, and a tear formed in the corner of her eye.

"Ho there, little one," boomed a familiar voice to her left. She scrabbled to sit upright and scooted across the cart away from the voice, wincing at the pain that bloomed across her shoulders.

The affable face of Horst peered over the side of the cart, smiling at Ursula. He was still chubby in the face, but the way his uniform hung from his frame showed how much weight he had lost since he had been deployed. Beneath the soot and dirt twinkled a pair of blue eyes that Ursula thought reminded her of the old legends of Sinterklaas. He pushed his helmet back on his head and reached for his water bottle, which he handed to Ursula. Gratefully, she grabbed it with both hands, the warm, oddly metallic tasting water sluicing down her throat and over her dry, chapped lips, giving her instant relief and causing her to shudder a little with pleasure.

Presently, they stopped in a small clearing for the night, and Ursula sat in silence as she watched the soldiers set up camp. Mayer studied a map with puzzlement in his eyes as Horst lit the fire. Two others, Brandt and Winter, foraged for food and water, the pair of them all but mute. She looked at their scared faces, boys in the uniforms of men, and thought she was about the same age as the pair of them, there or thereabouts. She watched them closely, their timidity surprising her. They flinched at any sound and seemed on permanent edge.

The Allies are closer than Mayer had admitted to her, she guessed. As she watched, she felt a prickle on the back of her neck, as if being watched. She spun around fast and saw the ratty visage of the fifth soldier watching her with a smirk on his cruel, thin lips. Wiesel, the others called him. The Weasel. He was sat on a fallen tree, one of his ubiquitous foul-smelling cigarettes clamped in the corner of his mouth.

"You are barking up the wrong tree with those boys, my pretty dove. You can have a real man instead," he sneered, his high reedy voice setting her teeth on edge. He pulled himself up to his feet and started towards her. She hated him.

"Pretty little dove like you, you don't need to be messing with those boys, not when I can show you what a man can do." He was small and wiry, and much older than the others, yet still only a basic soldier.

She turned her face away quickly, shuffling towards the back of the cart as surreptitiously as possible. Brandt and Winter were not in sight, obviously gone back into the forest for more wood. Horst and Mayer both had their backs to her, engrossed in their respective tasks, unheedful of Wiesel's advance.

"How old are you, my dove?" he cooed, now stood at the foot of the cart. She snapped to face him, trying to look as brave as possible.

"I am seventeen," she spat.

"Seventeen," he sighed. He leant on the side of the cart, removed his cigarette from his mouth and examined the glowing coal at the end with a squint, blowing on it gently. Without looking up, he added, "Seventeen years is a long time to leave a field unploughed, my little dove. Maybe tonight the farmer should tend to his duties."

Ursula recoiled in horror and tried to push herself further away, deeper into the clutter that filled the cart.

He glanced up and grinned, his uneven teeth coated in a brown patina from the cigarettes. While the others tried to keep a semblance of hygiene about their persons and, indeed, she imagined Mayer looked as pristine as the day he stepped out of officer academy, Wiesel was dirty. He glanced towards her, his expression quickly turning to a leer.

"Spoils of war, my little dove. The way it has always been, the way it always will be. Would you deny a brave soldier, fighting for your fatherland, some comfort on a cold night?"

"Wiesel. Stop." A voice filled with command came from Mayer. Ursula looked around with relief. He was stood, now only ten metres away, glaring at Wiesel. Horst stood with him, and she saw anger in his eyes, anger which transformed him from a chubby smiling fellow, the very picture of affability, into a big man filled with rage. She could see him tense his fists, and he started to move towards Wiesel before Mayer placed a restraining hand on his chest. Wiesel raised his hands and smiled.

"My apologies, Unterfeldwebel." He bowed in mock supplication. "I did not realise this was a resource the officers could access before us poor enlisted men. My apologies."

Mayer scowled. "This young lady is not a resource, soldier. She is a citizen of the Reich, and we are to protect her from harm. Now step away from her, and if I catch you speaking to her again without being spoken to first, I shall have you clapped in irons the minute we get to Berlin."

"If there's a Berlin left by the time we get there," grumbled Wiesel, but he turned away and walked into the forest.

Ursula smiled her thanks at Mayer, who ignored her and returned to his map.

"Little one, would you like to help with the fire?" Horst called across. Ursula found that she did, and she traipsed across to help him. In silence, the two worked on the fire, first getting it lit, then placing water on to boil. Ursula felt secure next to Horst, and the mundanity of the task helped with the loss she was barely coming to grips with.

Presently, Brandt and Winter returned with a brace of rabbits and some wild mushrooms, which, added to some of the herbs looted from her village, Horst started to turn into a surprisingly aromatic soup. As it bubbled on the fire, Ursula's stomach roiled inside her and she realised how ravenous she was. Darkness drew in and the accursed drizzle relented, and Ursula found a large boulder near the fire flat enough to sit on while she waited for the soup. Soon the soldiers finished their tasks and joined her, first Horst, then Winter and Brant, seemingly joined at the hip.

Finally, the light faded enough that Mayer put away his maps and joined them. Wiesel was the last to come to the fire, slouching from the frees barely five minutes before Horst declared the soup ready. He sat directly opposite Ursula, and in the gloom the fire made his eyes glitter as he watched her, like a snake watches a mouse. The soldiers all held their mess tins forward greedily, as Horst ladled out the delicious smelling broth. He had retrieved a bowl from the cart for Ursula, which she numbly recognised as her aunt Klara's fruit bowl, but she said nothing. The soup was incredible, the meat from the rabbit gamey and delicious, and all of them were silent as they ate. Some bread was brought from the cart, and they all tore a hunk and passed it between them, mopping up the grease from the rabbit flesh that lingered at the bottom of their bowls.

Satisfied, they all relaxed after the last drops were eaten. Horst accepted the compliments on his cooking with humility, praising Brandt and Winter for their superior hunting and foraging skills. The two boys smiled shyly, and Brandt rolled a cigarette which he shared with Winter. Wiesel had smoked throughout the meal, but he delved into the depths of his pack and brought out a bottle of kirsch, which Ursula quickly recognised as the one her father had put away for Xmas eve. It was half gone already, but Wiesel made a big show of passing it around while basking in his own magnanimity. Ursula took a swig, the fiery burn heated her throat and exploded in her belly most pleasantly. She thought maybe she should be crying, crying for her loss, crying for her situation, but she found she couldn't, and doubted she could ever cry again.

The bottle passed back and forth as the evening wore on. She listened to the soldier's stories as the fire warmed her bones. The heat made the burns on her face tingle, but it wasn't uncomfortable and the reassuring sounds of the trees she had grown up amongst felt good. Ursula felt almost human, for the first time since they had found her. Winter was first to tell his tale, explaining to Ursula how he was supposed to be studying philosophy, how just a few months ago the Reich had demanded even the students fight, how he found himself out here, cold and alone, until he joined Mayer's unit and met Brandt. Brandt told his story next, he was nineteen, older than he looked, and had grown up near Vienna.

His handsome boyish face nearly crumpled into tears as he recounted his first days in combat, how the only thing that got him through the horror was his friendship with Winter. Winter's hand drifted to Brandt's thigh as he told this story, squeezing gently in support. Ursula noticed, noticed how it lingered there a little too long. After finishing his story, Mayer reminded Brandt that he was on watch in four hours. Brandt nodded, asked for another pull on the kirsch and said his goodnight. Winter stood up at the same time and declared he was going to get some sleep too. He followed Brandt out of the firelight, into the dark, to the area in the clearing where they had lain their packs side by side. She looked up and saw Wiesel grinning at her wolfishly through the fire. He spat into it, his phlegm sizzling as it hit the blazing wood.

"Told you you were barking up the ywong tree." He grinned.

Ursula gasped a little as the penny dropped.

Mayer looked at her with some degree of sternness.

"I do not trouble myself with the sleeping arrangements of my men, miss," Mayer said, lighting another cigarette. "What matters to me is their bravery and sense of duty, both of which have been front and centre in those two men. Irregular times call for irregular soldiers. Who am I to judge the men who put their lives on the line for me every day?"

"They will be judged, though. It's the pink triangle for those boys once the gestapo finds out about their 'friendship'." Wiesel laughed.

"They won't find out though, will they, Wiesel? Not if you want the rest of us to keep quiet about all the Wehrmacht bodies you've looted over the last month or so," Horst said coolly, not looking up from the fire.

Wiesel began to say something in return but decided better of it, deciding instead to glare darkly at the embers.

The darkness drew in as Horst told her his story next, and his tale suited him; a poor twenty-two-year-old farm boy who had married his childhood sweetheart at nineteen and was desperate to get back to her and the baby that grew inside her. Ursula noted how his eyes glassed over at the mention of his soon-to-be expanded family, and she liked him even more for it.

Mayer leant forward and threw a small branch on the fire, sending sparks dancing up to the stars, Ursula watched them whirl, the comforting resinous smell of pine filling her head. She glanced around the clearing and saw that the darkness was already hiding where Brandt and Winter slept, and that all but Wiesel had shuffled closer to the fire. He was just on the periphery, the flames illuminating his face but the rest of his wiry frame enveloped in the gloom. She had slid from the boulder now to be closer to the fire, and sat on the ground like the others, her back resting against the rock.

"The temperature is dropping. I will fetch you a blanket," Horst said, as he lumbered to his feet and gingerly picked his way to the cart. The others sat in silence as his grey outline rummaged around for a moment or two before moving back into the lit circle of the fire. He handed Ursula an attractive crocheted blanket, what was once surely the pride of one of her neighbours' bedrooms, now trailing in the leaves and slightly singed around one edge. She thanked Horst and draped it around her shoulders. Horst smiled and reached for the kirsch bottle, now almost drained, and took a pull.

A sudden crack, so slight in volume that if any of them had been speaking it would have been missed sprang from the north of the clearing. Instantly, Mayer sprang to his feet, his pistol unholstered and pointed in the direction of the sound. Wordlessly, he gestured to Horst and Wiesel and the two clambered silently to their feet. Horst crept forwards, his pistol in his hand now too, while Wiesel slipped into the darkness and made his way towards the sound in the dark periphery of the trees.

Shortly, both men were lost to the darkness, but Mayer remained still as iron, his gun arm extended and completely unwavering. Without moving his eyes from where the sound came from, he motioned Ursula to be silent. Ursula held her breath, her scared eyes straining into the gloom to see any sign of Horst or Wiesel. Just when she thought she was going to pass out through lack of oxygen, the two soldiers came back into view. She let out a relieved gasp as they walked into the fire lit area, both holstering their Lugers, Horst shaking his head. At last Mayer relaxed, his arm falling to his side, but Ursula noted that he alone didn't put his gun away.

"Nothing, Sir," Horst explained. "No sign of anyone." Ursula was shocked to see how the men had gone from an easy-going fireside chat to soldiers in the blink of an eye.

"Good. It would be wise to remain more vigilante, though," Mayer said, finally returning to his seat. "We have no idea how far the Allies—"

"It's not the Allies that have you rattled, there's not an Englishman within three hundred miles of us. Stop this pretence," Wiesel sneered, interrupting his superior.

"Silence!" barked Mayer, but Ursula could see he was rattled for the first time she had known him.

"You brought her along, she deserves to know the truth." Wiesel gestured towards Ursula. Mayer looked to Horst, whose expression was the very definition of 'I don't like him, but he may be right.'

"What…What is it?" Ursula found her voice, and the moment he saw her scared expression, Mayer realised he had to tell her everything.

With a big sigh, Mayer leant backwards and put his face in his hands. After a few seconds, he looked up and looked Ursula straight in the eye. She could see fear there. Mayer reached out blindly and Horst slapped the bottle of kirsch into his hand. He finished half of the remainder in a big gulp, his body involuntarily shuddering at the strength of the spirit.

"We don't know what it is. That's the simple answer. But Wiesel is correct, the Allies are nowhere close." He spat into the fire, the alcohol remaining in his saliva sizzling and popping as it hit the flames. He looked at Ursula and registered the confusion on her face. "Okay, maybe I should start from the beginning."

All four of them moved closer to the fire, even Wiesel seemed to crave the companionship of the others. Horst placed another branch on the fire, the warmth almost instantly blooming on Ursula's tight red face. She huddled closer, enveloped in the blanket as Mayer reached for a cigarette which he lit from a flaming twig plucked from the blaze.

"Almost four months ago, at the very end of the spring, we started to lose men in this forest. At first, the regional commander was not worried. Patrols go missing, it happens. So he sent extra men in, bolstered the patrols, gave strict instructions to keep an eye out for the lost men." Mayer took a smaller drink this time and looked at the bottle as if for the first time. "I have always disliked chenies," he said, almost to himself, "but I do enjoy kirsch." He took a draw on his cigarette and continued, "Soon though, these patrols themselves started to disappear. The regional commander assumed that there was a desertion problem."

"And who could blame them for deserting?" glared Wiesel. "The war is all but over and men want their homes."

"But they weren't deserting," continued Mayer, ignoring the interruption. "Soon the issue became problematic enough that the commander was called back to Berlin to explain. Now, this forest of yours," Mayer attempted a smile at Ursula, "this forest here is part of a great and ancient forest, that stretches almost unbroken across Europe. What do you think happened when all the regional commanders were gathered together in Berlin?" Mayer didn't wait for an answer. "All of the zones that fell in the forest area, all of them, were suffering a huge amount of desertion." Mayer finished his cigarette and flicked it into the fire. "High command was baffled. Then, they started finding the bodies."

Ursula drew her knees up to her chin under the blanket. The night had got darker as well as colder, and for the first time the forest she had grown up in, known all her life, was becoming a place to be afraid of.

"A patrol was found buried in a shallow grave. All six men had every joint in their body broken. Yet there was no blood. Not on the men, not on the ground. Huge great weals around their throats led us to believe that they had been strangled."

Ursula pressed her back against the rock behind her, a shudder travelling the length of her spine. Horst was staring into the fire, his face expressionless. Wiesel was picking his teeth with the point of his knife, feigning indifference, bravado even, but Ursula could see he was rattled.

"So now we knew what to look for," continued Mayer, finishing the kirsch with a shiver. "Sure enough, the missing soldiers started to appear, all in the same state as the first. Joints snapped, strangled, tossed in a shallow grave and not a trace of blood anywhere. No open wounds, no gunshots, nothing." He lay the empty bottle on the grass beside him. "Always the whole patrol, and never any survivors." Horst stretched and rumbled to his feet.

"Excuse me, I must piss," Horst announced to the three. "I will check the perimeter while I am at it." Mayer nodded in thanks at this. "Wiesel? Could you see if there's any more kirsch in your pack? The night is cold, and the forest is dark," Horst said, and without waiting for an answer stepped towards the trees. He was swallowed by the darkness in just three steps.

"That was the last of the kirsch," Wiesel lied, making no effort to move from his spot by the fire. Mayer was absentmindedly plucking blades of grass from around him, flicking them into the fire.

"At first, the high command ordered the patrols to be doubled, they wanted whoever was doing this to be caught. A few weeks later, the disappearances had increased, and still there was no sign of the culprits." Mayer continued.

"So the officers and high and mighties did what they usually do," spat Wiesel venomously. "And decided to ignore it. Patrols were cut to bare bones. The poor devils that were left started to vanish faster and faster until the forest was almost abandoned."

"Quite so," agreed Mayer. "But then, a few weeks ago, the tides of war turned against our beloved Reich."

"The war turned months ago," muttered Wiesel to no-one in particular.

"And the Fuhrer began recalling troops to defend the homeland," continued Mayer, ignoring the interruption. "For some, like us, that means a few days traversing the forest before we can get to a transport hub to get shipped the rest of the way to Berlin."

"The high command actually showed some common sense for once." Wiesel lit a cigarette as he inched closer to the fire, his shoulders hunched against the cold. "While not officially recognising the forest was haunted," at this Mayer shot him a glance of warning, but Wiesel continued nonetheless, "they did at least have the decency to fill us poor cannon fodder in on what was happening here and across the region."

"But this makes no sense at all," blurted Ursula, "I have not left my village in months, and we have no disappearances, no-one went missing. My father travels to other towns on business, and he never once mentioned anything like this."

"That's part of the riddle," Mayer said, nearly smiling. "Villagers, hunters, trappers, any non-combatants, completely untouched. Not a soul missing. There was even a case where one of our patrols met with a group of travelling musicians and actors. The patrol offered to travel with them for a day or so, which they did, but the day after they parted ways, the patrol was never heard from again. The musicians were unharmed and could not recall a single thing out of place during their trip through the forest."

All three looked into the fire for a minute, before Ursula broke the silence. "So what—" She started.

"What is killing our men? I have no idea," Mayer finished for her. "There is no official statement from the generals. Obviously though, the soldiers, well, nobody is superstitious like a soldier."

Wiesel let out a contemptuous snort. "Or the generals have no common sense, and the soldiers do."

"Be that as it may," Mayer replied, "officially, we do not know what is causing it."

"And unofficially?" asked Ursula.

"Unofficially, my little dove, most of us soldiers believe this forest is haunted by the ghosts of Rome's dead legions," Wiesel spoke in a dull monotone, intending to scare. "Legionaries were slaughtered by their thousands in the forests that stretch across the fatherland. The Germanic tribes treated the invaders with cruelty and brutality. It is the spirits of the maltreated dead, left to rot amongst these trees."

Ursula raised her hand to her mouth in shock.

"Well, that's one theory," smiled Wiesel, warming to the attention. "My friend swears it is the Krampus, if you can believe that."

Ursula could indeed, the childhood terror of the Krampus was still fresh in her young mind.

"But the officers, well, the educated men, they have a different theory, right, Herr Unterfeldwebel?" Wiesel looked through the fire at Mayer, who was lighting another cigarette.

"Yes, I know what you are referring to, Wiesel," Mayer said, his voice sounding tired. "Some men, especially those with closer ties to Berlin, well, they say the Fuhrer has been dabbling in the dark arts, that he has been using the old ways of the land to try and win the war, but he met his match in Churchill, who is far more knowledgeable in the ways of the blood, the soil. They say in desperation, our Fuhrer awoke something dark and powerful and old in these forests, something that didn't want to be disturbed. Now it stalks these forests, taking any who bear the mark of the Reich in payment for his mistake."

Ursula shuddered. She knew, of course, that these forests were older than people, and she knew that if you wanted to stay safe, it was wise to perform some little ritual every now and then, a ritual that looked harmless but the forest accepted and appreciated. Her father had hung iron around their doorway, for instance, to protect the family. That had not helped much with a direct hit from a British bomb, she thought bitterly.

"So there you have it," Mayer said, leaning back slightly. "The full truth, and the reason why the men were so eager to bring you with us. The more superstitious amongst them, the boys and Horst, they thought you would be some kind of charm, an amulet to protect us." A sudden look of worry leapt across Mayer's face. "Horst has been gone a while now, hasn't he?"

Wiesel looked up, and even by the firelight, Ursula could see all the colour had drained from his face. The cocky weasel had been replaced by a terrified lamb.

Mayer climbed to his feet and unholstered his Luger, his hands shakier now, whether it was fear or the kirsch, Ursula couldn't tell. Wiesel did the same.

"Wiesel, go look for Horst. Go quietly. Take no light. I will go and wake Brandt and Winter and then help the search," Mayer whispered in a hoarse voice. Wiesel nodded, his face a mask of terror, and he slipped out of the light and into the trees instantly.

"You wait here." Mayer tried to smile at Ursula, but all she could see in his face was horror. "I will wake the boys and get one to sit with you while we search. You will be safe by the fire. I am sure old Horst has just got himself lost."

Before she could reply, he had reached into the fire for a stick that was glowing at one end. Ursula thought he looked like a wizard holding a wand as he held the glowing tip in front of him and stepped out of the light and into the dark. The glow was visible for no more than three seconds before it was swallowed by the night.

Ursula shuddered and drew the blanket around herself. The fire suddenly seemed very low and the night seemed very dark and cold. She tried to almost press herself into the rock she was propped against, as if she could hide inside the great old stone.

Abruptly, Mayer burst from the darkness at a sprint and dropped to his knees in front of the fire. His face was contorted in a rictus of terror and he looked close to tears.

"They're dead. They're both dead. Strangled." He gasped.

Ursula let out a gasp and struggled to her feet. "We must go, go now. Get up," she said to him, and started to reach out a hand to him. Mayer didn't move, he looked at her, then a point behind her, his eyes widening in dread as he fell backwards and staffed to scrabble away, desperately squirming a retreat in the dirt. Ursula looked puzzled, then, faintly, she felt something, as if a great presence were stood directly behind her, but silent, stealthy. Then the world, mercifully, went black.

Jeetu looked up as Basav entered the clearing. He dragged two of the pigs behind him, one foot in each of his gigantic hands. Jeetu noted that Basav had the same look of exhilaration on his face he always had after a successful hunt, beneath the sheen of exertion.

"How long until the female awakens, Brother Jeetu?" Basav asked.

"I think I applied enough pressure to give us ten minutes until she awakens, Brother Basav. Will that suffice?"

"I think so, Jeetu, if we work quickly and Kali smiles on us."

"I can't imagine she would do anything else, Basav." Jeetu smiled. "This was a fine hunt in her honour. Tell me though, is it wise to leave this little one? If she finds some more pigs to protect her tomorrow, she could lead them to this place and they would only be a day behind us."

"You know the wishes of Kali, Jeetu," Basav began, a tone of admonishment in his voice. "No females, no musicians or fakirs, no Brahmins or the sick shall we offer to her."

"Kali be praised," Jeetu replied automatically.

"Kali be praised indeed." Basav smiled. "I think the British will be pleased with our hunting tally this time out, do you agree, Jeetu?"

"I cannot see how they will not. The price of our temple's survival after the suppression was to assist them in their wars, and I would say we have done that admirably. The pigs are too afraid to step foot in this forest and the British army is only days away," Jeetu said. "Will we return straight to our temple after this, Basav?"

"I think not, Jeetu." Basav smiled. "We will be sent back to the base in England where Flight Lieutenant Lee of the SOE will find us another mission, I am sure." Jeetu smiled at this. He liked the tall Englishman, Lee, with his deep voice and crowded teeth. The special operations executive treated them very well, and Lee himself was a kind, fair officer. "Shall we finish up, Jeetu?"

Jeetu smiled in agreement and set about his work. Firstly, he left the clearing and returned a minute later, the body of Brandt slung over his shoulder. He dumped it unceremoniously in the pile that Basav had started. Horst on the bottom, then Wiesel. He then left to gather the body of Winter. In the meantime, Basav had lifted the body of Mayer over to the rock that only minutes before Ursula had been sat against. A huge purple welt covered the throat of the young officer, a testament to Jeetu's skill with the rumal, the bright yellow sash that was the sole weapon of the thuggee. Basav lifted Mayer's left arm to the crest of the rock, where he carefully applied his massive strength either side. After a few seconds of exertion, there was a ghastly crack and the elbow was disjointed. Basav was quick and skilful, never causing the pig to spill a single drop of blood as he shattered its joints. First the elbows, then the shoulders. The knees required twisting the corpse so the pressure could be exerted on the side. Finally, the spine was snapped in the centre and the body tumbled to the forest floor like a rag doll.

Jeetu dumped the body of Winter onto the ground, then gathered up the boneless body of Mayer and walked twenty or so paces into the forest to the spot where, almost two hours ago, they had used the sacred pick to dig the shallow grave, as Kali wished. Years of strict training had given the men eyes that were accustomed to the poor light, and Jeetu had no problems finding the spot. He hefted the body of the young man into the pit, where it tumbled and finally lay, contorted.

While most of the rules the thuggee followed were intended to honour Kali, a few were in place for practicality purposes. The guru who had taught them both had explained the necessity of the graves, to stop jackals uncovering the bodies, but the breaking of the joints made the remains much smaller and therefore a much shallower grave was required. *No jackals here, though*, thought Jeetu to himself as he made his way into the clearing. He was surprised to see Basav was nearly finished in his task, the bodies of the two youngest pigs were both already broken and piled up. Basav grunted as he lifted the body of the skinny older one onto the rocks.

"Brother Jeetu, this one appears to have survived my rumal," Basav called over. Jeetu looked in surprise and walked over to where Basav was stood. Peering closer in the dim light, he could see the chest of the man, this fellow who looked like a mongoose or a rat, rise and fall almost imperceptibly.

"Should we finish the job?" Jeetu asked, his hands already moving to his waist to untie his sash.

"I think not, Brother Jeetu," replied Basav. "We must respect Kali. If she has decided this man's karma is bad enough to endure what comes next while still living, who are we to argue?" With that, Basav gripped the arm of Wiesel and with a second of pressure, the joint snapped. Wiesel's eyes shot open immediately and he tried to scream in agony, but due to the colossal damage to his throat, all that issued was a gravelly croak.

Jeetu looked on with interest as Basav roughly dragged Wiesel over the rock and in a matter of seconds, snapped his other elbow. This time Wiesel's scream was so animalistic that flecks of blood were spat out with it. Wiesel thrashed from side to side, his horrified mind seeing nothing but the two brown faces, one a mask of concentration, the other filled with horrible inquiry.

"Kali must want you to suffer, pig," grunted Basav as he pushed Wiesel off the rock, only to grab him by the left leg and drag him back on. "I wonder what you did to offend her?"

The horror of his situation had sunk in to Wiesel, and he started to thrash and kick out at his tormentors. Jeetu jumped forward to help secure his free right leg, while Basav easily restrained the other on the rock. With a gasp of exertion and an audible pop, Basav separated the knee.

Wiesel screamed and screamed, but the hoarseness made it barely audible. He started to babble in German, pleading for mercy.

"What do you think he says, Brother?" asked Jeetu.

"I have no idea. I never bothered learning the language of these pigs, I assumed I would only meet dead ones."

They both laughed at this, a rich, deep chocolaty laugh that made Wiesel stop his pleading and look at them in shocked dread. Then he was roughly turned over his right knee on the rock, his face in the leaf mould. The fecund stink of the forest assailed his nostrils and leaves and dirt filled his eyes and mouth for a brief second until the agony pierced his skull and his right knee was separated.

Wiesel felt rough hands on his shoulders as the smaller of the two men dragged him across the rock. He felt the sharp crest in the centre of his spine, saw the stars stare down on him, uncaring. He pissed himself at that moment, as he felt the pressure from the massive hands on his torso. The tip of the rock dug in, dull and blunt and the pressure built. It became harder and harder to breathe and Wiesel's mind snapped in terror a second before his spine did, ending his agony.

Ursula woke up to find everyone gone. Her throat was tender, and the fire had burnt out. Of the soldiers that had accompanied her, there was no trace, but the cart containing the remains of her village was untouched. She sat up on the grass for a minute, shrugged to herself, then gathered herself up and started to go about the long task of taking the cart back home.

A Stupid Old Tradition

Ben knew something was amiss as soon as he walked into the kitchen. His mother sat at the tatty Formica table, back as straight as iron, her eyes glassy with tears. Her hair was scraped back, as usual, grey showing in the roots of what had once been a thick blonde mass. Both her hands rested on the tabletop, cradling a mug of that awful cocoa shit she insisted on drinking every December. The ubiquitous half full ashtray sat within reach, as usual.

Ben grunted a greeting, slinging his backpack in the general direction of the hook on the back door before heading to the fridge. Ben scowled at the radio, its tinny speaker letting him know that Roy Wood and Wizzard really did wish it could be Christmas every day. He chanced a glance over his shoulder and was somewhat surprised to see his mother was still gazing off into space. *Silly old cow*, he thought. She needs to pull herself together.

"Why is there never any fucking food in this house?" He turned from the fridge to glare at his mother. She didn't acknowledge him, didn't even look in his direction. Ben slammed the door of the fridge, hard.

"Ben, sit down, please." His mother's usually small and reedy voice contained an unexpected hint of steel.

"Oh, what is it now?" Ben huffed angrily. "I really don't have time for this shit, I have homework to do."

For the first time since he had entered the house, his mother looked at him.

"Is that so, Ben? Sit down, please." His mother's Austrian accent immediately rubbed him up the wrong way. She had lived here in England nearly twenty years, why the fuck does she still sound like the Terminator? Ben's mother reached for the pack of Benson and Hedges next to the ashtray, pulled one out, clamped it in her teeth and lit it with a cheap lighter. Ben noticed how much her hand was shaking as she performed her little ritual, worshipping at the altar of the great god cancer. She pointed to the other chair and looked away again as smoke curled from her nostrils and drifted lazily to the yellowing ceiling.

Ben let out a great dramatic sigh and dragged the chair out from under the table, its rubber feet scraping across the lino. He sat down heavily in the chair and leant it back on its rear two legs, which caused it to creak alarmingly under his weight. Ben was a big fifteen-year-old, he had inherited his size from his father, but his blue eyes and blonde hair were mirrored almost perfectly in the woman sat before him.

"Do not lean on the chair, you will break it, we only have two left," his mother snapped sharply. The other two had been broken just over a month ago, on Halloween, smashed by Ben himself in a rage at his mother's petty bureaucracy. Not that they needed any more than two, they never had any visitors, not since moving to this shithole six months ago. Actually, the visitors and houseguests had pretty much dried up when his father died, almost a year before that.

"God, fine," Ben huffed at her and reset the chair. "What do you want?"

"Your teacher, Mrs Hardcastle, called me today." She looked at him calmly enough, but Ben could see tears starting to well in the corners of her eyes.

"Ah, fuck. What lies did that stupid fat bitch tell you this time?"

"No lies, I think, Ben. She told me you had not attended school for a week until today. A week. Where have you been?"

He knew his time was up. It was too far down the road for lies or excuses this time.

"I was hanging with my mates. I hate school. What the fuck do I need fucking physics for?"

"But you went in today?" His mother's eyebrow arched in inquiry.

Ben started to rub the scuffed knuckles of his right hand.

"The boy is in the hospital, Ben." His mother looked at him, the tears starting down her face in earnest now.

Ben tried not to smirk, but couldn't help himself. He quickly looked down at his lap, hoping his mother would think it an act of penance and not see the smile on his face.

"His parents have agreed not to get the police involved this time out of respect for your father's memory, and the memory they had of you as a boy before all this happened. But this is the last time, Ben. The school says you will be permanently excluded next time you break a rule."

They probably didn't want the police involved because the beating was over money their precious son owed him for weed, thought Ben, but nevertheless, a wave of relief flooded over him.

"So, no worries then?" Ben asked, starting to lever himself up from the table. The halfwit DJ on the radio was ecstatically reminding his listeners that today was the fifth of December, only nineteen days to go before inflicting 'Mistletoe and Wine' on them.

"Stay where you are." The sharpness in his mother's voice took him aback a little.

"What now?"

"Today I went to the off licence, to buy some schnapps so we can put out a glass for Sinterklaas like we always do." Ben's stomach fell. He knew where this was going. "And what did I see, there in the window, Benjamin?" She pronounced it in the Germanic way, Ben-yah-Mean. Ben hated it, but had enough self-preservation to keep quiet.

"I saw a photo in the window, of my only child. A photo declaring you are banned from the shop for stealing."

Ben risked a look up. His mother had gripped the mug so tightly her knuckles were white. She visibly shook with anger.

"It wasn't me, it was Steve and the others, they stole some vodka, I didn't even know they were going to do it—"

"LIES! STOP THE LIES!" Ben's mother shouted over him. As she stood up from the table, the backs of her skinny legs bumped the chair and it toppled backwards, coming to rest at an angle against the worn kitchen cupboard doors.

"You are a thief. Plain and simple," she hissed at him, a bony finger trembling in accusation.

Ben looked at her, horrified and afraid at first. Then something grew in him, some anger, frustration at the unfairness of it all. Something snapped.

"Oh fuck off, you self-righteous bitch!" Ben leapt up, his chair falling backwards to mirror his mother's. "The offy can afford it. And if you had given me the money like I asked, I wouldn't have had to steal it, would I! So, you're as much to blame as me."

"What? How dare you. We have no money, not for vodka, not since your father died. You know that. That's why we moved here."

"You have money enough for your precious fucking fags." Ben reached across the table, towards the cigarettes. His mother reached a hand to protect them but she was too slow. Ben snatched them from the table and leant back in his chair, hand holding the packet outstretched behind him, a cruel smile on his face.

"Ben, please, that's a full pack, I can't afford anymore until Tuesday."

"I know." Ben grinned as he crushed the gold cardboard completely.

With a sob, Ben's mother slumped into her chair. Ben looked at her with contempt, her bowed head, pathetic and crying, as he crumpled and destroyed the cigarettes in his hand, dropping the wreckage on the table.

"I think we're done here," he said, a note of mock joviality in his voice, as he rose from the pitted table and left the kitchen. "I'll be in my room playing Xbox if you need me."

She cried and cried. His footsteps echoed up the stairs, almost in time with Andy Williams declaring that it was, despite evidence to the contrary, the most wonderful time of the year.

Ben looked up as a tentative knock came from his door. He paused his game and smiled a little. Pathetic. He knew she'd come begging for forgiveness. Her weakness angered him, rendered him almost nauseous. His father had been a great alpine bear of a man, a mechanic by trade who worked hard and drank harder. He and Ben's mother had moved from Austria to England in ninety-eight for work, and Ben had come along five years later. He had been a rough, rugged man, but a devoted father. His notorious devil-may-care attitude was a source of his popularity, but after he died early last year, his family had discovered that attitude had spread to concepts like saving money and life insurance.

"What now?" Ben grunted angrily at the door. "You come up here to accuse me of something else? Blame me for Brexit?" Actually, Ben was struggling to keep up the facade of aggression. Two hours in his room playing Xbox and enjoying some truly spectacular weed had mellowed him immensely.

The door creaked open a crack and his mother's worried, tired, mousy face appeared.

"Ben, I was wondering if you would like to put out the things for Sinterklaas and Krampus, like we always do?"

Shit, was it December fifth already? Actually, Ben had always liked the tradition of Sinterklaas, it was one part of his heritage that he embraced. He had fond memories of waking up on the sixth with a shoe filled with delicious German chocolate, and shivered in recollection of how his mother and father had terrified him with stories of the Krampus, that wild, hairy demon that dragged bad children away screaming, their fate unknown but final.

"God, okay, if I must." He sighed dramatically.

The door opened wider and his mother stepped tentatively into the room. He watched her face as she surveyed his tiny room, the beer cans used as ashtrays, the clothes strewn everywhere. He smiled inwardly as he saw her nose wrinkle with disgust as the stench of the dank weed hit her. A few months ago, he wouldn't have dared to smoke in his room, now he didn't even bother to open the window. She spotted he was watching her and an unsteady smile crept onto her lips.

"Thank you, Ben. You know how much your father loved this night. It meant a lot to him. He loved the chocolate and he loved to tell you all the old stories of Krampus."

Ben lurched to his feet and instantly had to steady himself with the door of his cupboard. His source had not been lying, for once, when he had said this was some seriously prime shit, he giggled to himself.

"Yeah, I stopped believing in that stupid old shit years ago," Ben lied, "but if it keeps you quiet, let's get it over with."

Ben's mother's smile reached her eyes and became more genuine as she left the room, Ben following her.

"Oh, you must believe in the Krampus, Ben, he comes in the night and takes—" she began excitedly.

"Yeah-yeah, he takes the bad kids away, never to be heard from agaaaaaaaaain," Ben intoned in funereal tones as he followed her down the stairs into the living room. The room was crowded, the furniture from their old house far too big for this new, smaller place. A sofa faced a television, with a coffee table between. A sideboard held two large framed photos, his mother and father on their wedding day, his father lifting his mother into the air, both of them with huge smiles across their faces, the other of the three of them, Ben maybe five or six years old, sat in front of a huge log fire on one of their many trips back to the old country.

Ben could see his mother had been busy during the couple of hours he had spent getting baked in his room. The box of decorations was crammed into a corner and the Xmas knickknacks he remembered as a child were starting to find spaces on shelves. Ben's mother fished in the box and came up with a pair of old leather baby shoes, and her face creased in a smile as genuine as Ben had seen in months as she handed them to him.

"Would you like to put your shoes by the front door for Sinterklaas?"

"Jesus, Mother, I'm a bit bloody old for all these stupid old superstitions, don't you think? Why don't we just cut out the middle man and you give me the chocolate now. Anyway," he added for good measure, "I think someone would steal them in this neighbourhood." He knew this would hurt her, their diminished station being a great source of pain for her, but he was past caring.

His mother's smile evaporated and was replaced with her usual crestfallen, beaten dog expression.

"They are not stupid superstitions, they are important. Your father and I wanted you to keep your traditions, your heritage."

Ben looked at her and shook his head pityingly. But some of that Sinterklaas chocolate would go down a treat, and if he had to wait 'til tomorrow, who cared. Thinking about it, he could just sneak down and get it after the old bag went to bed, and scoff the lot while indulging in some more of the quite astonishing weed currently stashed in his room.

"God, okay, if it really means that much to you, I will." He all but snatched his baby shoes from his mother's hand and marched the few steps to the door, flinging it open and placing the shoes on the doorstep. The cold December air hit him hard and almost took his breath away. There was damp in the air too, and Ben would not be surprised if they got some snow before Xmas this year. He slammed the door behind him and trudged back into the living room. His mother was stood in the tiny gap between coffee table and sofa, the box full of decorations on the table, his mother's tiny frame almost toppling into the box as she rooted around.

"Aha!" she cried in triumph as she held a large, pale branch above her head in victory. "Here it is, the oak branch!"

Ben sighed impatiently. "Jesus, Mother, it's just a bit of bloody wood." He squeezed himself onto the sofa, pushed the box to one side with his feet and reached for the TV remote.

"Oh, it is not just a piece of wood, it's the branch from the—"

"—tree in the churchyard in the village you and Dad grew up in," Ben finished in a bored monotone. "Blah blah blah, the holy oak branch that parents of good kids hang on the door to ward off ol' Krampus. Shit, woman, I didn't believe when I was nine, I'm sure as shit don't believe in this crap now." He looked into her eyes and took a small piece of sadistic pleasure in watching her face crumple in sadness, and found himself mildly disappointed that she composed herself before the tears actually came. She dropped the oak branch wordlessly onto the sofa and shuffled from the room. Ben feigned disinterest and switched the TV on.

As he flicked through the channels, he heard clinking from the kitchen, and a few seconds later, she appeared with a decorated tray. On the tray sat a plate, and Ben was both surprised and pleased to see three lebkuchen, the delightfully spiced festive biscuit on there, alongside a small glass that contained an almost oily, clear liquid Ben knew to be peach schnapps. His mother gently made room on the sideboard for the tray, smiling as she did so at the photo.

"There, Jurgie," she almost whispered, "the gifts for Sinterklaas." And she kissed the tips of her fingers and brushed them against the wedding picture, a gesture Ben had seen a thousand times. Turning to her son, she added, "Maybe you are right, Ben. Maybe it is time for us to stop with all this baby stuff. You are a grown man now, and maybe I should treat you as such." Ben put down the remote and looked up in surprise.

"Here." She opened the sideboard door and pulled out a small carrier bag. "Here is the chocolate I got for you for tomorrow. You may as well have it now."

Ben greedily snatched the bag and dumped the contents on the table.

"What the fuck is this?" He glared at her angrily, sifting through the four or five bars of chocolate. "Twix? KitKat? Where's the good shit? The German stuff?"

"I could not afford it this year, Ben," she answered, not meeting his eyes.

"Oh for fuck's sake, you really are useless," Ben shouted angrily, as he climbed to his feet, stuffing the chocolate bars back in the bag. "Where did you get this shit? The all-night garage?" His mother didn't meet his angry glare as she started to place things back in the box, carefully laying the old branch on the top.

Ben threw the remote on the table with a clatter, stood up and made for the door.

"I see you still had enough money for your stuff, though," he spat angrily and pointed towards the tray. "Tell you what, I think I will take this to make up for it." And he grabbed the glass of strong smelling liquor, held it up to the light in a mock toast and drained it.

He looked at her, hoping for a reaction. He got nothing but a look of defeat. He sneered, slammed the glass down and went back to his room.

He finally heard the silly cow go to bed around midnight. *She cried more than usual tonight*, he thought to himself. Oh well, not his problem. He switched off his game and lay back on his bed. *A quick smoke and then sleep*, he thought. Tomorrow was a school day and he probably should go in, at least until the heat died down a little. He placed his hands behind his head as he stared at the ceiling. Christ, he remembered Krampus Nacht as a kid, he thought, sat on his dad's lap, thrilling to the tales of the demon of Xmas, his dad smelling of schnapps and Swarfega, his huge hands holding Ben tight as he shuddered in delicious terror, his smiling mother hanging the old branch on the front door, making them all cocoa.

A boom from downstairs shocked him from his reverie. He sat up instantly. *Stupid bitch forgot to shut the door properly and the wind has blown it open*, he thought. Well, he was buggered if he was going to get up to shut it.

"Mum, you left the door open, you daft old cow."

Nothing from his mother's room. The flimsy walls in this place meant you could hear a mouse fart from downstairs, so she must be asleep.

"MUM. DOOR!" he bellowed. This time he heard it, a muffled sob from her room and some words, sounding like German.

"For fuck's sake," he complained and started to get out of bed.

The door slammed shut with an almighty bang. Ben heard what sounded like a picture falling from the wall and breaking from the impact. *Oh well*, he thought, *it's blown shut.*

"Don't bother yourself, you useless old bitch, it's blown shut now," he bellowed through the walls. The sounds of his mother's sobs increased and her gibbering in that horrible language intensified.

"Es tut mir leid. Es tut mir so leid, mein Sohn," she sobbed, over and over. Ben had never bothered with German, but he remembered a few words. *Mein Sohn* was my son, his father used to say that when he had too much to drink and Ben sat on his lap. '*Ich liebe dich mein Sohn*, I love you, my son.'

A creak from the stairs made Ben swing his legs off the bed fast. What the fuck was that? Some Chav from the neighbourhood had got in when his stupid mother left the door open, he thought, but deep down, deep in some primal part of his fogged mind, he knew that's not what it was. He knew, as the sobs and cries from his mother's room increased, he knew, as the goatlike stench hit his nostrils. He knew, as the creaking sounds slowly climbed the stairs, getting closer and closer. He knew, as his door burst open, and there he stood, the devil of Xmas, hairy and horned, barely contained by the doorway.

He knew, as he screamed and evacuated his bowels in fear, crying on his bed, as the beast dragged him by his hair and threw him in the sack, the sack that stank of shit and piss and children's last terror. He knew as he screamed and begged his mother for help, for forgiveness, for the branch of oak. He knew, as his head hit every step on the way out the door. He knew.

A Guest for Dinner

Merton let the door slam behind him as he entered the hallway. His home was warm, the central heating made a welcome respite from the cold drizzle that fell incessantly outside. He stepped out of his shoes and fastidiously placed his keys in the bowl on the side. He hung up his coat carefully on its peg and stretched out with a groan. It was good to be home. He breathed in deeply through his nose and caught the smells of domestication—meat cooking in the oven, vegetables boiling on the stove. He smiled and started down the narrow hallway towards the kitchen. The living room door was adjacent to the stairs, and he paused in the doorway. The TV was on, blaring colours and noise. Sat, directly in front, cross-legged, was Cassie.

"Hi, Cassie."

The girl did not acknowledge his greeting.

"I said, hi Cassie," Merton said, louder now to be heard over the noise from the telly, a note of annoyance creeping in.

"Hi, Bob," the teenage girl said, with nothing in her voice, her eyes never straying from the braying mob on the screen. Merton looked at her, her dark hair and school uniform, looking very much like her mother. He started to say something to her, to rebuke her for her rudeness perhaps, but decided he wasn't in the mood to repeat that particular row with his stepdaughter today, he was in too good a mood, and so he continued to the kitchen, wordlessly shaking his head.

"That you, love?" The familiar chirpy voice of his wife, Dawn, greeted him as he stepped through, her back to the door as she rooted around in the fridge for something.

"Yup, it's me," Merton said as he sank into the chair with a groan. The kitchen table was already set, and he was happy to see a freshly poured glass of beer in front of him. He gave a soft grunt of pleasure as he reached for it and took a deep swallow.

"I poured you a beer, love," Dawn said without turning around, as she delved further into the depths of the fridge. "Where the bloody hell is the mustard?" She muttered to herself.

"Thanks," said Merton. "What's for tea?"

"I thought I'd make us a cottage pie." Dawn turned around to smile at him, mustard triumphantly raised in her hand. "Found it." She placed the condiment on the table and kissed Merton lightly on the top of the head. "How was your day?"

"Busy," Merton replied. "I think we won the Ronson contract."

"That's wonderful news!" beamed Dawn, her face all smiles.

"Yeah, it was hard work but worth it. Should double the turnover in under three years."

Dawn smiled encouragingly at him as she fussed with the place settings, moving knives and forks fractions of millimetres until they passed her unforgiving scrutiny. Merton took another swig of beer and relaxed, the stresses of the day slowly starting to melt from his knotted muscles to be replaced by a warm sense of contentment. He was, on the whole, happy with his lot. Business was steady if not spectacular, and his homelife was the same. There was some trouble with Cassie, of course, but that was to be expected with a teenage stepdaughter, and if he were to be completely honest with himself, part of the shift in their relationship was his fault.

He knew he was noticing her in a different way now, now she was blooming in the early flushes of her womanhood, the resemblance to her mother impossible to ignore, a resemblance free from the lumpiness of middle age, a copy fresh and young and lithe. He had not found Dawn attractive in years, pretty much the moment he had snagged her, he had started to go off her. Fortunately, there were plenty of younger ladies who still found him attractive, whose athleticism and lust for life were the perfect antidote for Dawn's good-natured homeliness. Merton shook his head unconsciously, trying to shake the thoughts out of it. He refocused on the room and saw his wife looking him dead in the eye. For a horrible moment, he thought that his countenance had somehow betrayed him, had displayed his confused feelings for her to read, but the hopeful shy smile of anticipation on her face caused him to almost sigh with relief.

"Well?" He asked after a beat or two, his eyebrow cocked in inquiry.

"Well?" Dawn laughed, nervously, Merton thought. "Aren't you going to ask me about my day?"

"Oh, of course, how silly of me. How was your day?" Merton smiled supportively. Inwardly, he rolled his eyes as soon as he had finished the sentence. He had no interest in the minutiae of his wife's day, did not care what was on special at the supermarket, or who she saw at the bank, or what her sister Marie had called up to tell her. It had to be one of those, it was always one of those.

"You'll never guess who rang me this afternoon."

Bingo, thought Merton. He was too good sometimes.

"Erm…was it the Archbishop of Canterbury?" He asked with a look of feigned innocence.

Dawn laughed, dutifully, like she had not heard this joke a thousand times before.

"No, silly!" She gave a playful swat at his arm.

"Mother Teresa? Enid Blyton? Sir Cliff Richard? Ian Botham?"

"No, no, no and no." Dawn giggled obligingly.

"Oh, I don't know, I give up, was it…Marie?" He reached for his glass again, smugly.

"No." Dawn sat down at the table, and Merton saw the nervousness was back.

"No?" Merton asked, surprised. It was always Marie. His hand paused, his glass held to his lips.

"No." Dawn looked downwards, towards her lap. Her fingers fiddled nervously with the edge of the tablecloth. Without looking up, and in a very faint voice, she added, "It was Jeff."

Merton's eyes widened involuntarily and he slowly, carefully, placed his glass back on the table.

"Jeff? Your Jeff?" he asked. He could feel the colour had drained from his face, hear the slight tremble in his voice.

Without looking up, Dawn nodded her head.

They sat in silence for a moment, the only sound the shrieking of the over-excited host coming from the television in the room next door.

"Well?" Merton squeaked, coughed, and then continued in his normal voice, "Well? What did he want?"

"He wanted to talk." Dawn got up from the table and turned to face the sink, her back to him.

"Are you sure it was Jeff?" Merton asked.

"Of course, I am. I was with him for nearly twenty years. I know what his voice sounds like"

"What did he have to say? Any explanation where he's been these last two years?"

Dawn slumped forwards, her elbows resting on the edge of the sink. "It was a bad line. A very bad line. He was crying the whole time, he said he only had five minutes. He said he was lonely, he missed me, he missed Cassie."

Merton fell silent, shakily reached for his glass, finished the beer in one swallow. It couldn't be Jeff. All of the relaxed feelings, all of the contentment fled Merton. He felt the stress bunch in his shoulders, he felt nausea in his stomach, he felt a headache coming on.

It couldn't be Jeff.

Jeff had taken the split with Dawn hard, and who could blame him. His childhood sweetheart, lured away by Merton, his best friend. For a year or so after Dawn had left him, he called continually, begging her to take him back. Suddenly, completely out of the blue, Cassie received a letter from him saying he was going to visit a distant relative in Canada, he wouldn't bother them again, and not to look for him. Cassie had been devastated at first, she and her father were very close, but after a while she settled into the new life with Merton, her father not forgotten, but certainly not intruding into their lives in a daily fashion. Merton used Jeff's desertion as ammunition, pointing out how he couldn't have ever really cared for Dawn and his daughter, not if he was willing to run off without a trace.

But it couldn't be Jeff.

"Have you told Cassie?" Merton asked, his mouth dry despite the beer.

"Not yet."

"Did he say what he had been up to these last two years?"

"No. Like I said, he was crying a lot, he said he was lonely and cold. He said it was always dark without us." Dawn turned to face Merton and he could see tears beginning to form in her eyes. "He was so sad, Bob. So sad. It made me feel like hell for what we did to him."

Merton silently got up from his chair and walked to the fridge. He pulled a fresh can of beer out and opened it, taking a huge swig before sitting back down, the niceties of using a glass forgotten.

Dawn turned again, her back to him, and he could see her shoulders heaving as she tried to suppress her tears, tears that he knew were coming. He tried to calm himself. *Be rational*, he thought to himself. After a second, the emotional fog started to lift and he began to think with clarity. It wasn't Jeff, couldn't have been Jeff, so who was it?

"Look, love," he began, "you said the line was bad. Is there any chance it could have been someone pretending to be Jeff? Maybe as a joke? One of Cassie's friends perhaps?" Or the boyfriend of one of the young ladies he had been dallying with lately, he thought to himself.

Dawn shook her head vehemently. "No, it was Jeff."

But it couldn't have been Jeff.

"Maybe you misheard the person? Maybe you had a bad dream or something? Fell asleep on the sofa? You have been stressed lately, jumping to a lot of conclusions. Remember how mad you got at my secretary Claire calling me about work last month?" Claire had not been calling about work, Claire had been calling about a pregnancy scare, but he had bluffed his way through that one. The close call had not given him cause to stop the relationship, however, just to proceed with a touch more caution.

Dawn shook her head again. She turned slowly, her hand wiping away the tears that Merton knew were coming. "It was Jeff. I didn't dream it, I didn't mistake someone else for him, it was Jeff."

"It can't have been Jeff. You must have made a mistake."

"There's something else."

Merton raised an eyebrow quizzically. "Go on."

"Well, I felt so bad for him, so sorry, I told him to come over tonight, to see Cassie, have dinner with us. I knew you wouldn't mind."

Merton stared in stunned silence. "What?"

"He's coming for dinner tonight."

Three slow, deliberate thumps came from the front door. Merton looked up, horrified, but he couldn't move, his legs remained paralysed.

"I'll get it!" Cassie said from the front room. He heard her get to her feet, her light footsteps skitter across the carpet. Finally, Merton summoned up an inner reserve of strength and stood up, his chair falling backwards in the process.

"No! Stop!" he bellowed. "It's not Jeff. It can't be Jeff. I killed Jeff. I killed him and threw his body in the sea. I killed him, and I faked the letter. It can't be Jeff, it's not Jeff." Dawn spun around, her eyes filled with horror and disbelief. "Cassie!" Merton shouted. "Cassie! Stop!"

But as he shouted, Merton heard the familiar sound of the front door opening and felt the cold damp air as it rushed into the house.

"Daddy!" squealed Cassie, her voice happier than Merton could recall.

"Daddy?" Cassie repeated, this time pensively, as the stench of seawater, of rot, of dead things left in the cold lonely dark, drifted into the kitchen.

Richard Jones

The taller of the two sat himself at the bar next to the shorter one.

"Evening, Ted," greeted the shorter.

"Evening, young Stewart," responded the taller.

"Pint of the usual, Ted?" enquired Keith the landlord from his perch behind the bar. He didn't look up from his crossword.

"Lovely." Ted smiled. "You ready for another there, Stew?"

Stewart tilted his pint glass towards him and examined the inch of amber liquid left in the bottom.

"I think I could manage another, cheers," Stewart replied before emptying his glass.

Keith hopped from his stool and set about pouring both men's beers with a skilled and practiced hand. The two watched him work, his artistry with the pumps causing them to fall into a reverential silence. Presently, two perfectly poured pints of spitfire were placed in front of the two friends.

"Champion, thanks Keith," said Ted, fishing out a handful of coins from his pocket and counting out the cost of the round. Keith smiled at them both and put the coins in the till without bothering to ring up the sale. Taxman be damned, was

Keith's mantra, and he'd be buggered before he would help the fellows at His Majesty's tax office by recording every little thing. Let the grasping sods work it out themselves. Transaction complete, Keith brushed some imaginary fluff from his action slacks and climbed back onto his throne to complete his crossword.

The two lifted their glasses in unison and took a large swallow before carefully placing their glasses on cardboard beer mats that advertised a brand of beer neither had heard of and Keith didn't sell. Ted let out a satisfied sigh and slipped his jacket off his shoulders, draping it over the back of the barstool to match Stewart's.

"How's your day been then?" enquired Ted of Stew.

"Oh, you know, same old, nothing to report really. Is it still raining out? It was just starting as I got here."

"Nah, it was just a shower, I waited for it to pass before setting out, hence my slight tardiness."

Stewart seemed satisfied by this and the two men sat into an easy silence, punctuated only by the crackle of the fire and the tick of the pub clock. Ted took another deep draught of his beer, draining it to the half pint line.

"Actually, I read something in the paper today that may prove of interest," Ted said.

This pulled Stewart from his reverie, peering, as he was, towards the mysterious and unloved optics on the shelf, trying and failing to decode what the labels had printed on them under the dust. Decades he and Ted had drunk in this pub, and he had yet to see Keith pour a drink from any of them, save the brandy bottle at the end from which Keith would pour a free glass to his favourite customers on Xmas eve.

"Is there a particular reason we are speaking in the manner of a BBC newsreader?" Stewart asked, arching an eyebrow.

"Oh. Was I? Sorry," Ted replied. "Anyway, back to my news. I saw something that may come as a bit of a surprise to you in the paper."

"The local?" said Stewart, absentmindedly printing damp crescents on the bar mat with the base of his half empty glass.

"No, the Times," Ted answered. "Today's. Well, I was gobsmacked. Remember Richard Jones?" Stewart ceased his decorative efforts and looked at his friend.

"Jonesy? Of course. What's he been up to now? I haven't seen him in years."

"With good reason, it would seem. He's in prison."

Stewart turned his head towards his friend, his eyes wide with inquiry.

"Not only imprisoned, but the subject of a great deal of discussion in the offices of the lawmakers. Discussion as to whether we should bring back hanging, specifically for Jonesy, and Jonesy alone."

"What's this?" Keith had appeared magically behind the bar in front of them. Despite his outward appearance of calm capability, the landlord was a drama addict, and any gossip of any kind was almost guaranteed to drag him out from the depths of his crossword. His eyes flicked between the two friends, sparkling behind his spectacles in anticipation of the forthcoming juicy details. "Prison? Hanging? Who is this Jonesy of which you speak?"

"We went to school with him," Stewart began. "He was in our year. Nice bloke, we hung around with him quite a bit. Mad keen Spurs supporter, he was. We used to take the piss something chronic."

"Yeah," continued Ted. "He would come down the park with us, go around each other's houses, that kind of thing. He was just like us, normal kid. Absolutely brilliant goalie. Should've had trials but never did. Anyway, that all changed when we were, what? About fifteen?" Stewart nodded in agreement as he took a sip of his drink. "Fifteen. That was the summer he met, bugger, what was her name?" Stewart drained his glass fully and placed it on the mat.

"Cassandra. Well, she called herself Cassandra but her real name was just plain old Sandra." Ted drained his glass and placed it next to its twin on the bar.

"Another, gents?" asked Keith, but he was already pouring two fresh ones as he did. Ted and Stewart again fell silent as they watched the master at work. Keith placed them on the bar and took a fiver from Stewart in exchange, and after making change he encouraged Ted to resume his tale, which he did with pleasure.

"Cassandra, yeah, that was it. She was gorgeous. Goth chick. All black fringe and boobs." Ted took a sip and continued, "Anyway, he fell really hard for her, but she was way out of his league. So, to get her attention, he started getting into the goth stuff. Started wearing eyeliner, listening to the Sisters of Mercy, that kind of thing. Anyway, it worked, because they started going out together."

"Problem was," Stewart took over, "problem was, she was so good-looking, geezers would hit on her all the time. And she was a lady who loved the attention. And poor old Jonesy was such an ugly little spud that the only way he could keep her interested was to up his game on the goth stuff front. This worked for a bit, and we kind of stopped hanging out with him then as much. That was about the time he insisted we all called him Draven instead of Jonesy. Got a bit much." He paused for a drink and Ted seamlessly continued.

"Ugly spud seems somewhat harsh, but yeah, so anyway that worked for a while, but we all got a bit older and started hanging around in pubs and such, and she was now getting attention from men, proper, grown up men with jobs and that. Jonesy was powerless, and so he did the only thing that he thought he could."

"He killed her?" gasped Keith, hand to his mouth in shock.

"What? No! No, he didn't kill her. He got some books about black magic from the library and tried to cast a love spell." Stewart looked aghast. "Killed her?" He shook his head.

"Oh," said Keith in a small voice, hoping the others wouldn't hear the disappointment in it. "So, dabbling with the occult to try and get a girl to like you, sounds legit."

"Well, you have to remember we were all arsing around with the ineffable at that time. Seances in graveyards, Ouija boards, all that toot." Ted noticed Keith's eyebrow raised in bafflement. "It was the eighties," he added as explanation, and Keith nodded in satisfaction.

"So did it work?" Keith asked.

"Of course, it didn't. Magic isn't real," Stewart said, his glass en route to his lips.

"Well…" said Ted, uncertainty in his voice. "Anyway, we don't know if it would have worked or not, because after weeks of scavenging around town for all the ingredients, his mum went to tidy his room and found it all. Ingredients, occult symbols, the lot."

"She went mental," understated Stewart. "Well, she was head of the PTA and made tea for the young Conservatives. Did the flowers in church on special occasions too. She went Bertie. Chucked out all of his stuff and made him go for a meeting at the church with the vicar. After that, there was no more Draven, he was back to being Jonesy, and we saw a lot more of him. Cassandra dumped him almost immediately, went off with a married trainee welder called Steve or Dave, one of those names. Got knocked up in about a month, Dave or Steve or whoever went back to his missus before she even dropped the sprog, she and the kid ended up moving away."

"That's right," Ted said. "So old Jonesy was back, but he was really different. He was heartbroken, and it was all his mum's fault. And so, to spite her and her social aspirations, he started to pretend to be a black magic practitioner. Or so we thought."

"Yeah," smiled Stewart. "He was same old Jonesy with us, but you know, he started to drop Satan references into everyday situations around his mum just to wind her up. She'd sneeze, he would say 'Satan bless you,' that kind of juvenile stuff. He got right into it, torturing his poor old mum like this, to the point that he would do it all the time. His mum made him go back to the vicar and the vicar recommended a psychiatrist.

"The psychiatrist blamed the heavy metal records and video nasties that were prevalent at the time, and so his mum packed up and moved them both back up north, where her parents still lived. We lost contact really then for a few years, the odd letter or phone call for the first year or so, but that petered out. You know how it goes."

Keith did indeed know how it goes, and nodded accordingly.

"So, anyway, after about five or six years, I dunno, we must have all been in our mid-twenties, his mum dies and he moves back here. But now, he's worked out that a certain type of lady is fascinated by the whole Satan worshipping stuff, so he's pretending to be a Satanist to hit on girls. Brilliant scheme, really, when you think about it." Stewart looked at the emptiness of his glass and sighed. "It must be hot in here, my beer keeps evaporating before I get a chance to drink it."

Keith smiled and went about the business of refilling the beer glasses, while Ted and Stewart took the opportunity to take a wee in the pub's immaculate lavs. Break over, they all reconvened at the bar.

"So he wasn't a Satanist, he just pretended to be one to hit on girls?" asked Keith.

"Pretty much, or so we thought at the time," answered Ted. "He got the books back out from the library and learnt a few phrases and buzzwords. Like Stew said, he wasn't the most attractive bloke in the bar, so, you know, any little helps. And it worked, too, from time to time. Yeah, so anyway, this goes on for a while, then he gets a job offer back up north, too good to turn down, so he goes off again, and that's the last we see of him, pretty much. All this was maybe one or two years before you took over here." Keith took an already spotless glass from the shelf and started to clean it with the towel that permanently hung from his shoulders.

"Okay, so that's you up to speed, and where my knowledge of the story ends," said Stewart. Turning to Ted, he asked, "So, what did the paper say?"

"He wasn't making it up."

Keith and Stewart looked directly at Ted. Ted, revelling in being the centre of attention, took his time taking a long swig of his drink.

"Not a word. Apparently, he never forgot Cassandra, and one day a few weeks back, he turned up at her house after tracking her down, stark naked, covered in occult symbols painted all over his body in blood. He explains that he is now a master thaumaturge, a wizard of the highest rank. He tells her that he has cast a spell of dominion, and all are powerless to resist him."

"And was she?" asked Keith, wide eyed again.

"Doubtful, considering there's no such thing as magic." Stewart laughed, while motioning Ted to continue with the tale.

"She did exactly what you or I would do," said Ted, "when confronted by a naked man with Satanic symbols painted on their body in blood, declaring their undying love—screamed the bloody place down. Neighbour hears and calls the cozzers, but it's too late; by the time they show up, he has killed Cassandra and the kid. Not just killed, but hung them up over the banisters and slit their throats, collecting the blood in an assortment of jam jars and saucepans he's found in their home. The copper that nicks Jonesy says he was totally calm, collecting the blood, and in his interview blamed the poor quality of the blood which he used for the symbols on the spell not working. If he used his one true love's blood, he explained, it would've worked, and then he could bring her back to life.

"So the police go to his house, and find a pit in his basement. And in the pit are bodies. The oldest, at the bottom, are cats and other pets, things he thought he could get away with. The newest, at the top, were kids. So many kids. Furthermore, it turned out Dave or Steve never went back to his wife, old Jonesy admitted to bumping him off and hiding his body out in the woods. And then he told them about his mum." Ted looked at the rounded, shocked eyes of the other two, took a swig, and continued, "Her, he not just killed, but ate, over a period of about a month. When the police asked whether that was for occult purposes, for a spell, he just laughed and said no, that one was just for fun."

Ted sat back in his stool, smiling at the speechless faces of his audience.

"Wow," said Keith.

"Blimey," said Stewart.

"I know, right?" said Ted.

They sat in silence for a minute, Ted and Stewart drinking, while Keith stood polishing his clean glasses with a faraway look in his eyes.

"So, anyway, the coppers are all really intrigued by how calm he is and all that, and he tells them that he's not worried, as he has mastered the black arts, and he can escape anytime he wants. So the police say prove it, and he clicks his fingers, and—"

"He disappeared in a puff of smoke?" asked Keith.

"No such thing as magic, remember, Keith?" reminded Stewart.

"No, there was no puff of smoke. He just started screaming and acting bizarrely, still is, apparently. He had to be totally sedated. Started screaming he wasn't who he was, if that makes any sense. Police think it's a play for insanity but they're not convinced." Ted smiled.

"Hold on," said Keith, putting down his glass, "how can you have read in a paper this morning about stuff that's going on now? That makes no sense at all."

"Actually, he's got a point there," said a puzzled Stewart. "How was that in the paper?"

Ted looked crestfallen. "Bugger. I didn't think of that. Oh I wish you hadn't noticed that, Keith. You seem like a nice bloke. And I always liked you, Stewart." He reached forwards with both hands and grabbed Keith's ears firmly, then quickly smashed his face down on the bar. Keith's face hit his near empty glass which shattered, sending spears of glass into Keith's eyes and blood pumping onto the once pristine bar. Keith was dead before he hit the floor.

Ted, or the person that was inside him, whirled around to the shocked Stewart and drove a fist deep into his soft belly, causing him to double up in pain and crumple to the floor. He smashed Stewart's glass on the side of the bar and walked around behind him. Ted's fingers reached down over his Stewart's face and slipped into his nostrils. Pulling back sharply, he quickly slashed the smaller man's throat, sending yet more blood arcing through the pub, spattering the clock and sizzling on the fire. He dropped the glass on the floor and walked out of the door, into the rain which had just started again.

"I wonder if Spurs won tonight?" he said to himself, as he shut the door behind him.

Printed in Great Britain
by Amazon